Never Give Up

Skylar L. Hill

First Edition Published 2020 by Bob Scott Publishing

www.facebook.com/BobScottPublishing

ISBN: 978-1-952819-00-1

This is a work of fiction. All characters and events portrayed in this novel are fictitious and are products of the author's imagination and any resemblance to actual events, or locales or persons, living or dead are entirely coincidental.

Chapter 1

"Maddy, why do you keep falling?" I asked, being the curious little sister that I am.

"Lily, I have a huge recital in two days, and I need to get this move to perfection so I don't let my team down."

"I can do what you are doing. Watch me!"

As I reminisced about my childhood, the images of my sister and I practicing the Grand Jeté floated around in my mind. Being 16 years old now, that specific move is easy but when I was five years old it wasn't as easy as it looked. A Grand Jeté is a big leap in which your front leg is shooting out in the front, and your back leg is straight out in the back and you are high up in the air. Growing up and being surrounded by my sister and the art of dance is what I believe started my dancing career.

My mother always told me when I went to Maddy's dance recitals I would be clueless the whole entire time except for when she would do a Grand Jeté. Maddy always knew when I saw her complete a Grand Jeté to perfection because I screamed the loudest. Ten years later, nothing has changed, and I tell her how proud I am of her every chance I get, and how after high school I'm wanting to follow in her footsteps and become a professional dancer.

The only thing stopping me was truly believing in myself that I could do it. I didn't necessarily have the best coordination when I was little, but I was still determined to do what my sister did. I didn't want to give up, no matter what came my way.

The first time I danced was in kindergarten. My school started a program for girls my age who were interested. When my teacher told the class about it, I could barely hold my excitement. I ran home and told my parents. I figured they would allow me to dance since I was the same age Maddy was when she started dancing. My prediction was far from correct. The conversation with my parents didn't go the way I thought it would. The memory still saddens me as I remember that day.

"Mommy and Daddy! Look what I got from school! I want to do dance just like Maddy!"

The expressions on my parents' faces indicated disapproval. My mom shook her head, and my dad mouthed the word no.

"Lily, sweetie, I'm not sure dance is the right thing for you. I know you mean well and really want to do this, but we aren't so sure."

"Why, Daddy?"

"Lily, you have a habit of not finishing what you start. We don't want you to start this and then a week later come running to us, telling us that you want to quit."

"I won't, Daddy. I promise. I really want to do dance, and I'm passionate about it too."

"Let me talk to your mom and see what she says. Now go and play until dinner."

"Okay."

I ran to my room and waited to see what my parents decided. I was anxious to hear the results. To pass the time, I decided to do some dancing. I went to Maddy's room to dig through all her ballet CD's. Once I found one that I liked, I went back to my room. I had to dig my CD player out that I got for my birthday a year ago. I wanted to practice the Grand

Jeté. I was still young and didn't have long legs at the time, which made it harder. Maddy would help me whenever she had free time. Now what came next in that long evening was difficult for a six-year-old.

I tried to listen to what my parents had to say, but they were too far away, and I was distracted by the music. I turned it down so my parents wouldn't get suspicious of me eavesdropping. They were in the living room at the end of the stairs talking, but they still whispered so it made the task even more challenging.

I remember dinner wasn't at the usual time. It seemed like I waited for hours, but in reality, I only had to wait a little longer than any other day. Once I got called for dinner, I remember running down the stairs because I almost fell, I caught myself and landed on my feet. I wanted to know the answer to whether or not I could start dance. However, my parents kept me waiting until we finished dinner, but the conversation was one I will never forget.

"Lily, your Mom and I have discussed the issue. After talking it over and with your sister's opinion, we have decided that we will allow you the chance to dance. If you are serious about dancing, then you will have to practice for one hour after school at least three out of the seven days of the week. Do you understand?"

"I understand. Thanks, Mom and Dad!" I gave my parents a huge hug to show them how appreciative I was of them giving me the chance.

"You're welcome, sweetie," my parents said at the same exact time.

The next couple of days were easy to remember since I was excited about the opportunity, and I knew there was a good chance that my best friend Amiah could be dancing with me.

The next day, as soon as I stepped foot into the school, I saw Amiah running up to me. She talked fast to where I could barely understand what she was saying. I tried to get her to slow down so she wouldn't run out of breath and could actually speak. I had to grab her shoulders and hold her down. Obviously, Amiah was elated, so I allowed her to tell her news first.

"Lily, I'm doing the dance program!"

"I am too, Amiah!"

If my memory serves me correctly, Amiah was a fantastic dancer, so I knew she would have no problem doing the program. I wasn't surprised her parents allowed her to participate. When we turned our papers in, we got a schedule of when our practices and our meetings were going to be.

According to the paper, we weren't going to start any practices or anything for another month, but we were still given the schedule ahead of time so we could plan accordingly. I wanted to practice before dinner, so I knew what to do. I had an easy time learning them because Amiah came over after dinner to help me since her parents had an appointment to go check on how her unborn little sister was doing. Amiah's little sister was on her way in less than three months from that day exactly, and at the time Amiah wasn't excited about it at all. She had always been the baby of the family and received all the attention, but she knew everything was going to be different once the little one arrived. At the time, I was the baby of the family as well, so whenever Amiah would come over all the attention would be on us.

That night, I learned how to do a Cabriole. The specific move was a jump in which your legs meet in the front or in the back. One leg is extended first, and the other is lifted to meet it quickly before landing on the supporting leg. The night went fast because we practiced for two hours straight. In all of the craziness of dancing, I knew I was forgetting something that was required for school the next day. The only reason I knew something was off is because my parents came into my room with their faces as red as a tomato. In their hand was the reading log that I didn't fill out saying I had read for homework. I tried to lie about it and told my parents that I actually did do my reading, but I forgot to fill my log out. My parents knew better and could tell I was lying. To this day I'm still not good at lying.

I regretted not doing the reading because the next day in class we had a quiz over the material that was in the reading. Since I knew nothing about it, I got a big fat F.

My teacher called my parents to let them know. I knew once I got home my punishment was going to be atrocious since this wasn't my first time failing a reading quiz. That evening, my mother was the one who punished me. My father worked late which was good for me because my mother wasn't as harsh when it came to punishments. She grounded me for three weeks and told me I had to read the two chapters before even thinking about dancing. As a six-year-old, dancing was a lot more fun than homework. It took me forever to do what was required of me because I kept stopping and sneaking in a dance move or two, but I still wanted to practice dancing. Even though I knew how strict my parents were with me, I went against their rules and danced instead of going to sleep. I must have been making a lot of noise because my mom come into my room at ten that night and yelled at me.

"Why are you up this late? You have school in the morning! Now go to bed. If I have to come in here one more time, you are in serious trouble!"

After I got yelled at, I reluctantly went straight to bed.

After a month of practicing and getting all the dance moves down to a point, the day finally arrived - dance practices started. During school, I couldn't stop talking about how excited I was to dance. Amiah and I couldn't concentrate on anything our teachers told us to do.

When the last bell rang, Amiah and I were the first ones to pop out of our seats and run down the hall to the dance studio. We wanted to be the first ones so we could introduce ourselves to the teacher. Little did I know back then, trying to play nice and get on the teacher's good side wasn't always a good thing. Anyway, after the first five minutes of the meeting, we found out that the purpose of the day was mostly to discuss the rules and schedule of dance. It was hard for us girls to sit still. I think I might have started to daydream and not pay attention because Amiah had to pinch me. She told me the last ten minutes of the meeting we were going to have the opportunity to practice the first minute of the first song we were going to do at a Christmas recital.

As soon as my foot hit the front door after school, I was bombarded with questions about the meeting. Questions like; "How was dance practice? What did you learn? Do you like it? Do you think you are wanting to continue with it?" All of these questions overwhelmed a six-year-old who had a long day at school, and dancing made the day even longer. Surprisingly, dance could take a lot out of a six-year-old who never really experienced any type of exercise, or dancing besides the little bit she did with her sister. I slept well that night. I remember going to bed early that night after dinner. I didn't feel like practicing, even though I knew I made a promise to my parents that I would. When I was six though, I thought I could get away with anything and just make up for it another time. That other time was the next morning. I got up early and practiced to make up for the previous night.

My parents made sure I practiced every night until my first recital. I had to be honest with myself and say I did have nerves that entire day, even though I wanted to play it off like I didn't. I knew my parents didn't expect me to be perfect at my first recital or anything for that matter, but they did put a lot of pressure on me leading up to that night. They invited almost my whole family to watch. I knew they all held me to a higher standard since all I did was dance, but at the same time, I knew I wouldn't reach their standards. I failed many times at the dance moves while practicing even though they were simple ballet moves. All I could do was try as hard as I could as a little girl at the time. My family would be proud of me one way or another.

The recital is a memory like it happened yesterday. It was seven o'clock at night when the lights went down, and everyone knew it was time for the show to begin. I had a solo right after Amiah, so I knew I had to impress everyone, this way they knew a six-year-old could do anything they set their mind to. The stage reminded me of the Christmas season. There were red and green lights strung across it, a fake Christmas tree with presents underneath it, and fake snow coming down. Amiah and I wore matching red dresses. Red was my favorite color because it gave me confidence.

When it was time for my solo, I started by taking my left foot across my right foot and letting the music guide my way. At the end of my solo, everyone in the auditorium stood and clapped, even though the song wasn't over yet. I didn't know why, but I accepted it and continued dancing. I felt like a true ballerina that night. I couldn't believe I actually did well.

Right after the recital, my whole family took me out to get ice cream. In that moment, I knew they were proud of me. From that day on, dancing was the one thing I knew I was never going to give up on, and I knew I had to pursue my passion of dancing.

Chapter 2

As a seventeen-year-old, I continue to think about the times I was a part of dancing programs and activities my school offered. I auditioned for almost every musical or play that had dancing in it. It got easier the more I practiced. By the eighth grade, along with Amiah, I was one of the top students in my dance class. My teachers would ask me to help other students who were struggling, and who had a problem with some of the dance moves. Helping other students was the fun part, but it got me in some trouble down the road.

Since the first grade, I have struggled with my grades. It got to the point where I almost had to give up dance. My parents said I needed to pay more attention to my school work, and if nothing improved, there would be serious consequences. The thought of giving up the only thing I actually cared about scared me like nothing before. I knew there was only one thing to do...I had to get a tutor to help me.

I wanted to prove my parents wrong. I knew I had what it took to do well in school, as well as continue dancing. They said I had three weeks to do better, or I would have to give up dance.

When the three weeks were up, my parents had a surprise when they looked up my grades. They honestly didn't think I could improve, but I did. I had straight A's. Those didn't last though.

After Christmas break, my school decided to put on a play. Of course, there was dancing in it. I knew I had to try out. There was no question about it. I rehearsed day after day, for hours on end. I wanted to get the lead role. The day of the audition, I went in and tried my hardest, but I had a mental brain dysfunction before the song was over.

I started my routine, but in the middle of everything, my mind went blank on what to do at the end. I didn't think I was going to get the lead because of my mess up. The week leading up to the results had me anxious like going to the dentist. When the day came that the cast list came out, I ran to the auditorium where they had what I was looking for. I couldn't believe what I saw - my name at the top of the list. I got the lead dancing part with five solos in it. I was screaming while jumping up and down like a little kid, while all the other kids just smiled and went on their way.

Once I got home, I told my parents the good news. Their faces were red when they found out, but it wasn't because they were happy for me.

"Lily, there is no way you are going to be a part of the play. You have worked way too much to get your grades back up. We will not let you ruin them again. Sorry, but this one is out of the question. Academics are more important than dance. When Maddy started high school, we never had this problem. She was at the top of her class both academically and in dance. It is not the same scenario for you though."

"Dad, I can do both at the same time. I promise!"

"Lily Ann, I said no! My decision is final."

"Whatever! I don't care what you say."

"You're grounded!"

I was so furious with my dad, I yelled, "I hate you," at the top of my lungs. I couldn't understand why my parents were being unfair about the situation. Okay, so my grades were a problem before, but I knew this time was going to be different.

That night in my room, an idea hit me - a way my parents couldn't find out I was doing the play anyway.

The next morning before school, I lied to my parents and told them I had tutoring. I mentioned I would be done around five when in all reality play rehearsal would be done at four-thirty. By telling them five, it would give me a chance to change out of my dance uniform. I hoped this plan wouldn't backfire on me. With my luck, I would get caught, but I was still going to take my chances though.

I only had the rehearsal on my mind. I couldn't enjoy myself as much because all my focus was on the trouble I was bound to get in if my parents caught me. I got through it though.

When my dad picked me up is when the real challenge began. He asked me one question that could change the credibility. The question was "How was tutoring?" I honestly didn't have an answer. I tried to come up with something right away.

"It was good. I got all of my homework done. I also got some extra practice for my test." I stuttered my words and spoke fast because I was nervous. My dad knew something was up since I only did that when I was lying.

"That's weird, Lily. I called the school to make sure you made it to tutoring because Amiah's mom said she saw you outside with a bunch of girls dancing."

"I'm not sure why because I was at tutoring. Maybe she saw someone who looked like me, and assumed it was me."

"I don't think so, Lily. The school said you never checked into your classes for tutoring."

"Okay, I'll admit it. I didn't go to tutoring. I went to play rehearsal. I wanted to prove to you and Mom I could handle both the play and school. I couldn't let everyone down at school since I'm the lead. I am sorry. I know you are disappointed, and you are probably going to ground me again. I deserve whatever punishment you give me, but can I have one chance to do the play and keep my grades up?"

"You know what, Lily?"

"What?"

"I'll make you a deal. If you get an A on both of your tests tomorrow you can continue being in the play. Do you understand?"

"Yes, I understand."

The whole evening, I did nothing but study. There was no choice but to get an A on both of these tests. Everyone counted on me. I also went to bed early so I could get a good night's sleep. I wanted to be on the top of my game.

In my mind, I could see no flaws in going to bed early. Unfortunately, I was wrong. I was in such a rush to get to bed, I forgot to set my alarm to get up the next morning. My alarm didn't go off, causing me to be running late. My teachers were strict. If you weren't there on time for the test, unless you had a valid excuse, or you were in the hospital, you could guarantee you would not receive an A.

I went to wake up Mom to see if she could take me to school. I needed to make it on time.

"Mom, get up! I'm late for school, I need to get there for the tests."

"What in the world are you yelling about, Lily?" my mom mumbled under her breath.

"My alarm never went off. I overslept. I missed the bus. I'm not going to make it to class on time unless you take me."

"Lily, I'm not taking you. I work a double shift today. Plus, you need to learn your lesson of checking your alarms before going to bed. Time to be a big girl."

"This isn't fair! You usually take me to school if I'm late."

"Not this time, Lily."

If my mom wanted me to find a way to school, then I was going to do exactly what she wanted.

It was pouring rain, but I honestly didn't care. I grabbed my umbrella and started running. The school was about a mile and a half away through the city. There was no way I would be able to make it within twenty minutes. All I could do was hope for the best.

When I was about to give up, a familiar car drove up beside me. It was Amiah and her mom. She had social anxiety and it made it difficult for her to be in a crowd, like on a bus, without having a mental break down.

"Do you need a ride, Lily?"

"Yes, please. I missed the bus. I need to make it on time for the tests."

"Come on. We will give you a ride."

"Thank you!"

On the way to school, Amiah and I didn't do anything but laugh about play rehearsal and how I about fell on top of this boy. This is what happens when two best friends are together.

When we got to school, I had exactly three minutes to get to math class, but I made it. I was a step away from the door, and my teacher accidentally shut the door on me. I slipped my hands through, this way I could get all the way into class.

"You are late, Lily!"

"I'm not, Mrs. Geno. I was in the classroom before you shut the door. Therefore, I am on time." I thought I was pleading my case, but she obviously thought something else and scolded me in front of the entire class.

"You better lose the attitude, missy, or you will not be permitted to take this test, meaning you will automatically fail."

"Please. I need to take this test."

"Sit down and be quiet. I don't want to hear another sound out of you for the rest of the class."

"Fine!"

I listened and waited patiently. I was prepared. As the test was getting passed out, I was looking over my notes until I got mine. I usually did this with all my classes. I haven't had a problem with it until today.

When Mrs. Geno got to my desk she yelled at me because I had all my stuff out. She told me I automatically failed the test. I thought it was unfair. Amiah saw everything and stood up for me.

"Lily wasn't doing anything wrong. She was studying a little more before the test. Please, let her take the test."

"You know what, Amiah, you are right. I am sorry, Lily. I will allow you to take the test."

"Thank you. You won't be disappointed."

I had no idea what I witnessed, but it was amazing. Amiah always had this way of getting anyone to not be upset anymore. I got started on my test right away. I wrote a note to Amiah when it was only the students in the classroom.

Amiah, thank you for what you did for me. I don't know how to repay you.

I rapidly folded the note into a paper plane and threw it to Amiah. My aim usually wasn't good, but this time was different. It landed right on top of Amiah's desk. It was good timing too because when it landed, our teacher came back in. I could tell by the look on her face she was surprised everyone worked while she was gone because she said, "Wow! This is the first time I have left the room, came back, and didn't feel like I wanted to pull my hair out. Thank you!"

I was the second to last one done with the test. When I turned it in, I got a smile like never before. The only other time I saw our teacher this happy was when she started teaching at the beginning of the year.

This was her first year teaching, and she was ecstatic that she got the job since she had just graduated college the summer before. I went back to my desk and started studying for the science test. I felt confident that I got an A on the math one since I was prepared.

Mrs. Geno announced that we would know what we got on our tests before we left class. The thought of knowing before leaving class got my heart beating and kept me anxious. I read to pass the time.

The rest of the class went slowly. I thought I was going to have a breakdown because I wanted to know my grade. When the bell rang, I was the first one to hop out of my seat and run to get the test. I immediately handed it to Amiah without looking at it first. I wanted her to tell me if I should have been happy or not.

"Lily, I have some bad news for you."

"What is it, Amiah? Did I not get an A?"

"Look for yourself."

I took the paper, flipped it over, and about had a heart attack. I had gotten the A I had hoped for. I wanted to slap Amiah for allowing me to think I did horribly.

"Amiah! How could you pull such a mean joke?"

"I thought it would be funny to see your face, Lily. Relax. You got what you wanted. Now all you need to do is get an A on the science test, then you are golden."

"You are right, Amiah. All I need to do is focus. I can already dream about the lead role."

"You got this, Lily."

"Thank you, Amiah."

Science was at the end of the day, so I had six more classes to get through until I took the test. The day seemed to go as slow as humanly possible. It was killing my thinking. I knew the longer I went without taking it, there was more of a chance I would forget everything. I thought I was going to fail. Amiah kept reassuring me I was going to ace it exactly as I did with the math test. She was right. All I had to do was believe in myself. I had determination. Plus, science was my best subject.

When I got inside of my class, the test was already on everybody's desk. I guess it was going to take the entire hour of class. Mr. Rein wanted us to take advantage of all the time we had. He would even give me extra time if I truly needed it since I did have dyslexia. Some people it affects their spelling but with me, it just affects my reading.

The test wasn't hard. It only took me half of the class to finish. I continued reading my book after to focus on something other than the results. Mr. Rein usually didn't give back anything before the end of class times. It took him a lot longer to grade than most teachers. I did ask if he could grade my test though. I was willing to stay after class if he needed me to.

At the end of class, Mr. Rein had already graded my test. I about jumped out of my pants when I saw my grade. I received an A! I was especially happy because not only did I get an A, but I got bonus points as well! I couldn't believe my luck.

When I got home, I showed my parents the grades. To celebrate, they decided to take me out to dinner. We went to get sushi at this little seafood place down the street from us. I was in my happy place when I was there. The thing I liked most were their endless lobster legs. During dinner, my parents kept telling me I would be going to tutoring before I could go to play rehearsal. I had to continue to get A's in school. I reluctantly agreed because I knew it was the only way I could continue my passion.

The next few weeks went quickly and smoothly. The play was starting to come together. I was able to keep up with school, and everything in my life was going perfectly. I was all excited about the play until something bad happened.

I was at rehearsal and I knew I was having a hard time with the Fouetté. This move was a pirouette which was performed with a circular whipping movement of the raised leg to the side. I usually got close to perfection, but there was always one thing I could do to make it better. Well, on the day of the first performance, we were going through the whole thing. There was this one boy. He was doing his part when he accidentally went too far to the right. I went to do my solo, and I accidentally bumped into him and fell.

"Watch where you are going," the boy pushed me again after I got back up.

"I didn't mean it. You need to watch as well. You went too far. You needed to be three steps further from me. I know exactly where I am supposed to be. Apparently, you don't."

"Excuse me. I do know where I need to be, now you better get up, you lazy girl, so we can keep practicing."

"Whatever you say!"

I tried to get up but I couldn't. I fell right back down whenever I stood up. My dance teacher came rushing over and offered assistance. One of the other dancers went to get ice. I was told to elevate my ankle for the rest of the afternoon and see how I felt once I came back later that evening. I needed to feel better, this way I wouldn't let anyone down. I had to not limp so my parents wouldn't suspect I was hurt. I didn't want my understudy to take my place. I was given an ankle brace to keep it still.

Later that evening, once I got to the stage, my teacher came over to see how I was feeling. I lied and told her it didn't even hurt. She believed me. I went on warming up. I knew after three minutes it was going to be a long evening. I was limping, but I was determined to finish what I started. The play started at seven o'clock.

When the music started, I did my first solo act. It went absolutely amazing if I do say so myself. Everyone cheered so loud that there was an echo. Even though I did good, my ankle was hurting like nothing before. The play lasted until nine o'clock. At the end of the play, I had to come clean to my parents. The pain was unbearable. When I got off the stage, I limped to my parents while stumbling. My dad caught me right before I fell flat on my face.

"What's wrong with you, Lily?"

"My ankle," I said while tears came running down my face.

"What's wrong with it?"

I pulled off my shoe and lifted up my leggings. It was worse than before. It was black, bruised, and swollen.

"What in the world happened?"

"I fell today while rehearsing and twisted it."

"I think you did more than twisted it, sweetie. Why didn't you tell us earlier? Why did you dance even though you were hurt?"

"I didn't want to disappoint anyone. Plus, it didn't hurt until after I started warming up and the play was about to begin."

"Lily, you have to start taking better care of yourself."

"I know, Dad. I'm sorry."

"We are leaving right away to get it checked out."

Within fifteen minutes we were at the hospital and waited to get checked out. We had to wait about a half-hour after we got there to get called back.

"What brings you guys to the emergency room this fine evening?"

"I twisted my ankle while dancing."

"I see. I am going to push on your ankle. If it hurts tell me to stop."

When he touched my ankle, I screamed like someone was murdering me.

"We are going to do an x-ray to see if there are any fractured bones."

I was sweating, shaking, and crying while I waited for the results. My parents tried to keep my mind off the pain by telling me stories of me dancing when I was younger. When the x-rays finally came back, they revealed I had four fractured bones. I did not like the news one bit.

"Lily, I'm afraid to tell you that dance is off the table for a while. You have to be on crutches for at least eight weeks."

I didn't know what I was going to be able to do with myself.

Chapter 3

As the eight weeks continued, all I wanted to do was get back to dancing. If I could get to the four week mark, I could get off the crutches and walk in a boot. I still wouldn't be able to do any dancing though. The closest I got to returning to my passion was attending practices. Amiah helped me a lot with getting around by carrying my bags, this way I wouldn't hurt myself more. The day I planned on getting my boot off and start dancing again, I received some bad news from my parents. My mom sat me down before my doctor's appointment and expressed some news she knew I wasn't going to like.

"Lily, sweetie, I have some news for you."

"What is it, Mom?"

"Your dad got another job opportunity."

"That's great!"

"Before you get all excited, here is the bad part of the news. The job is in France."

"What? This means we will have to move. There is no way I am leaving! I am settled into dance, and I'm about to head off to college in a few months."

"I know, Lily. Both your dad and I are sorry we are putting you through this. The reason I am telling you now is that two weeks from today will be your last day at school. I already emailed the school and told them about the situation. We will be enrolling you at Lycée Janson de Sailly in Paris. It is the top school in France."

"I don't care if it has the best ratings there is. I don't want to go!"

"I know, Lily. This was a hard decision for both your dad and me, but the decision is final. Our family needs this. It will help provide for our family even more than we can now."

"This isn't fair." I stumbled out the door and fell to my knees crying. Right at that moment, Amiah and her mom pulled up in the driveway. I had forgotten Amiah wanted to come with me to get my boot off. Amiah needed to be told the news. She was like me when it came to bad news. My prediction was right. Amiah broke down crying when I told her.

"Lily, you can't leave me. The dance team and I need you."

"I know, Amiah, I'm just as heartbroken as you are. I wish I could stay with you, but my parents aren't going to allow me."

"I'm going to miss you, Lily. You are my best friend. I don't know what I am going to do without you."

"It will be okay, Amiah. We can still call, text, and FaceTime. We will never lose contact with each other. Maybe, on the holidays or breaks from school, one of us can fly to see the other. Plus, I bet you and I would have a blast in France. Especially in Paris, France. We can always go see the Eiffel Tower. Maybe those French classes will come in handy."

We both laughed hysterically. We lost track of time. We didn't realize we were going to be late for my appointment if we didn't leave right away. My mom got us in the car and we were on the road. It only took us ten minutes to get to the doctors. We had seven minutes to spare.

Once we got to the doctors, Amiah and I were talking about some dance fails we had done over the years. Now, when we look back on them, it's even more funny than when they first happened. We were so stuck on the stories that we didn't realize the doctor was calling me back.

I was so excited to get my boot off, I accidentally put so much pressure on my bad foot that I gave a screech.

"Lily, even though you are getting your boot off, you still have to be careful."

"I understand, Dr. Bainer."

After a couple of minutes of exercise, it was time for the boot to come off. My mom thought it would be funny to play my favorite ballet song while the doctor helped me. Once it was finally off, I hopped down and gave everyone a hug. I started dancing like it was my first time on stage. The good news about the boot made me forget the move, until the next morning.

At school, Mrs. Geno gave me all my tests back. I had no idea how I felt about leaving all my teachers. I loved Mr. Rein, and ever since Mrs. Geno started being nice, I loved her! I don't know how I was going to feel in two weeks when I actually had to leave.

At the end of the day, Amiah and I decided to walk home, so we could spend extra time with each other. We laughed and tried to remember all the memories we had made in the last seventeen years. We laughed to the point where our faces were bright red, and we had to sit on the ground since we weren't stable at all. When we got to the house, we walked in to see my parents were not at home. It was odd, usually my mom or dad was home when I was there. I did find something unusual, there was a package on the couch. There was a note attached.

Lily, here is a gift from your dad and I. We know this move isn't easy for you, or anyone at this point, but it is what we have to do.

23

We got you something that may help your eases, and keep communication with Amiah, or any of your other friends.

I unwrapped the present like a tornado spinning through a city. When I finally got the package opened, right in front of me was a new tablet I had been wanting for a year now. I was delighted my parents got it for me. Amiah and I spent the next few minutes setting it up to where I could Skype so we could video chat whenever we wanted.

My parents came home at around four-thirty. We still had a lot to get done for the move. We had to make sure all the furniture was going to be able to get shipped correctly. The things that were in the living room were getting shipped tonight, and we would use the chairs from the kitchen to watch television. We had to take Amiah home after dinner. Both she and I couldn't help but have tears running down our faces. The seats in the car looked like a river that had overflowed from a flood. I waved as we drove away from her house. The next two weeks went as slow as can be.

When the day came for us to leave, I cried the entire way to the airport. My mom tried to calm me down by explaining how this is a new start, no one knows us, and we have the opportunity to learn a new culture. Unfortunately, her technique didn't work. Nothing was going to change my mind or attitude about this situation. At that moment I wished there was a time machine I could use to go back and change the way my dad got this job opportunity.

When I boarded the plane all I wanted to do was run off, and go back to my old house where I belonged. I gave my parents the silent treatment for the entire flight. I still couldn't believe they would tear me away from everything I was comfortable with. I know the move was because my dad got a new job, but why did he have to accept the job, or have gotten a job that didn't make us pack up our lives and go somewhere that wasn't familiar? I didn't think it had anything to do with the job itself, but with the fact my dad was possibly offered a better position and pay, but only if he moved to Paris and completed the job. I was not certain this was why we were doing all of this, but it was my theory. I guessed I would never know until the time was right.

The plane ride was long and boring. I did have the new tablet I could play with, but there was no WI-FI, so I was limited on what I could do. When we finally landed in Paris, it was truly a sight to see. It was hot, humid, but had an astonishing display of lights in the far distant city. I knew it was going to take some time to get used to everything, but eventually, I would fall in love with my new home. We were greeted at the airport by my dad's boss who only spoke French. My parents didn't know any French, so I had to be the translator. I could understand the conversation, but it was weird.

"Bienvenue à Paris. Je suis ton patron. Je vais vous emmener chez vous. Cést la première mais la dernière fois que vous me verrez alors que nous changeons de place. Vous venez à Paris, je vais en Amérique." Which translated to; Welcome to Paris. I am your boss. I will be taking you to your home. This is the first but last time you will see me, as we are switching places. You come to Paris, I go to America.

My dad wanted to say; Thank you, sir, for this amazing opportunity. You will not regret it. America is beautiful. It has botanical gardens, historical museums, great city lights, and a funny theater. I know my family and I will love it in your country just as much as you will love ours. I translated and told the guy, "Merci, Monsieur, pour cette formidable opportunité. Vous ne le regretterez pas. L'Amérique est belle, is a des jardins botaniques, des musées historiques, de grandes lumières de la ville, et la théâtre drôle. Je connais ma famille et je vais ladorer dans votre pays tout autant que vous allez adorer le nôtre."

After the exchange, we got into the car, and his boss drove us to our new house. It was again another silent trip. On our way to the house, we went right by the Eiffel Tower. It didn't take long to get to our destination after we passed it. We were living about three minutes away. In my opinion, this was going to be a great experience. I have always wanted to see the Eiffel Tower, and now I was within walking distance from it. I couldn't wait to call Amiah and tell her. The new house was gorgeous. It was white, big, shiny, and had my favorite color roof tiles, blue! In my sight, this was perfection.

I went inside to try and get a hold of Amiah. There was only one thing stopping me. We didn't have any WI-FI. How could we not have WI-FI? I was depending on having it, I needed it to look up dance videos and communicate with Amiah. I had a distraught look on my face when my dad came in my room making sure I was unpacking and adjusting smoothly.

"What's wrong, Lily? Don't you like the house? Your reaction when we pulled up was like never before. I didn't think I would see a smile from you, at least not for a while since you were absolutely appalled we took you away from the only life you knew."

"I do like it here, except it doesn't have any WI-FI, and I am wanting to call Amiah to let her know I arrived. Why don't we have WI-FI, Dad?"

"I'm sorry, sweetie. We won't have WI-FI for a couple more days. Here in Paris, it always takes them a couple of days for them to come and install it. Until we can get WI-FI, you can go down to the library, which is right by the Eiffel Tower, and call Amiah from there. I'll take you in a few minutes after we bring everything in from the car. Do you want to come help, so you can get to the library faster?"

"Sure."

I was like the Flash to the car. I grabbed six boxes at a time. I knew I was going to fall, but I wanted to leave in the next five minutes. When my dad saw I was carrying a lot of boxes he tried to take some of the boxes away, so I wouldn't hurt myself again. I swatted his hand away. While doing that, I lost my balance, but I gained it right back. Being a dancer will help with things like balance.

"Slow down, Lily. You don't want to break your foot again before you start dance classes."

When my dad said that, I dropped all of the boxes because I didn't realize my parents were going to let me dance again. Dance back in California cost one hundred and fifty dollars, and I didn't think my parents could afford classes with the move.

"Wait! I can continue dancing? You didn't tell me this. I definitely thought that when we moved, I was going to have to give up dancing for good."

"No way, Lily. You were at the top of your class. We can't take that away from you."

I ran up and gave both of my parents a huge hug. I think they could tell I was excited because when I finished bringing all the boxes in, I forgot about going to the library, and dug through the boxes to find my CD player. I ran to my room so I could practice all my old dance routines. I was a little rusty on dancing since this was my first time dancing after getting my boot off.

At about seven-thirty, my mom came up to get me for dinner. Everything was still packed away, so we went out to eat. I was interested in trying some genuine French food. Who knows, maybe they had French fries. My mom about fell over on the floor laughing. I didn't know it was funny. I was assuming since they were called French fries, and we were in France, that they had some. We went to this restaurant called Au Bon Accueil. In my defense, it was really good. I was disappointed though, they didn't have any French fries or food I was familiar with, but all the same, it was delicious. I think I surprised my parents. I am usually a picky eater, and they could barely get me to eat anything they gave me, but tonight I ate everything on my plate. For dessert, I got this coconut cake, and it was to die for. The French actually had good taste in food.

When we got back to the house, it was time for me to get to bed since the next day was my first day at a different school. I knew the school in France was going to be totally different than the one in San Diego, California. I had a hard time falling asleep because I could imagine how my first day of classes was going to be. I tossed and turned the entire night. I fell off the bed once or twice.

The next morning, my parents had a hard time getting me up. All I wanted to do was sleep and hide away in my bed.

"Lily, time to get up. You don't want to be late for your first day of school, do you?"

"Go away. I want to be back in San Diego with Amiah and everyone else I know. I'm not French and people will recognize it."

"I know this is hard, but you have to go. You will fit right in. You know French, so this shouldn't be too hard."

"Come on, Mom. Can I finish high school online and then go to college in the fall?"

"Not an option, Liliana. Now get up!"

I immediately got up because I knew when my mother called me Liliana she meant business. The only reason I go by Lily is that on the day I was born, my great-great-grandmother, whose name was Liliana, got shot and killed in a drive-by shooting. I don't like the reminder of my name being after someone who was killed on the day I was born.

I had no idea what to wear today. I remembered my grandma bought me a new dress right before we left. It was one of those dresses that were flowy but didn't touch the ground. It was yellow with red stripes. When I got the dress on, I felt like a princess. I decided to make the best out of the day. I curled my hair and made sure I had all the paperwork I needed. My mom and I grabbed a bagel on the way to school.

When I first walked into the school, everyone was in uniform. My mom still had to pay for my uniform when I met with the principal. I tried to escape my mom's hand. There was no way anyone was going to make me wear the same thing as everyone else. I had my own personality, I wanted people to see it, but if I had to wear a uniform then there was no way I would be able to show it off for people to see the real me. I got halfway out the door before I ran into this six-foot guy who got in my way. When I looked back, my mom was furious. She grabbed me by the arm and dragged me to the main office. I was afraid of what was going to happen next. I was supposed to be meeting with the principal, but the only other person that walked in behind me was the guy I ran into.

29

"Hello, Miss. Liliana. I am Mr. Frankford. I am the principal here at Lycée Janson de Sailly. Here is your uniform. You will be required to wear this every day. If there is a day you arrive, and not in your uniform, there will be consequences. Do you understand?"

His voice scared me more then he did. "Yes, sir, I understand. You won't have any trouble with me." My voice trembled and shook. I obeyed and went to change into my uniform. It was a white top with a blue skirt.

When I first entered the bathroom, there was a group of girls staring at me. It looked like they had nothing better to do but terrorize the new student who was scared out of her mind. When I got out of the stall, they were still staring and making snarky remarks under their breath. I wanted to break down and cry. I couldn't show them I was a weakling, if I did it would give them more reasons to make fun of me. I went back down to the main office, where my mom was supposed to be, so she could say goodbye. I knew from the beginning that today was going to be torture, but I remembered Amiah once told me, "Fake it till you make it." I knew this phrase was going to come in handy these next few days.

I was saddened to see when I got to the office my mom had already left. I couldn't believe she didn't say goodbye. There was a girl in the office waiting for me though. She was going to be my mentor, and show me around the school. The only trouble was she only spoke French. I knew this would happen. I mean, I knew some French but was definitely not fluent in it. I needed to see if there was any possible way I could get either another student or a translator. I had to signal to the girl to be quiet since I forgot how to say stop in French. I went up to Mr. Frankford. My legs were trembling the whole way.

"Mr. Frankford. Is there any way I can get another student to show me around? I can't communicate with the girl you assigned me."

"I thought you could understand and speak fluent French. Your mother said you could on the enrollment papers. We put you in French-speaking classes only."

"I can speak and understand most French, but I won't be able to pass my classes if there isn't any English spoken. I don't know what happened with my mom and the enrollment papers."

"We will give you another person. Sit here for a little bit until we figure out your schedule, and put you in classes that are English speaking."

"Thank you."

As I sat there patiently, I got my tablet out and tried to set it up more. The school had some WI-FI, but it was weak. I was dying to get a hold of Amiah. All I wanted to do was talk to Amiah, she knew how to keep me calm. I didn't like this situation.

I sat in the office for an hour until everything was fixed. The new girl that came to the office for me looked oddly familiar.

"Hi. My name is Emmaline. Follow me. I will show you the school and what to expect."

She had a strict tone, but that wasn't the only thing troubling me. When I looked into her eyes, I realized she was a part of the group that was in the bathroom. I honestly didn't want to talk to her, but it looked like I had no choice.

"Hi. My name is Lily. I know you don't like me and that's fine, I don't like you either, so let's keep this simple. We don't talk, you show me around, and we will keep our own lives separate. How does that sound?"

"Sounds perfectly fine to me, Lily, or should I say, Liliana." The sly smile on her face made me think she was up to no good.

"Do not call me that!" I yelled so loud that Mr. Frankford heard me and came running towards me.

"What is going on here, girls? There will be no yelling in the hallways or anywhere in that matter."

"Emmaline called me by Liliana, and I hate the name. I go by Lily, always have and always will."

"This gives you no reason to yell, Lily. All you have to do is tell her not to call you by a certain name, and she will listen. Emmaline is one of our top students. Maybe her good behavior will rub off on you, eventually."

"Sorry, Mr. Frankford, but there is no way I am going to stay with her all day."

"You have no choice, Lily. Emmaline is the only one that can speak both French and English fluently. If you don't want her, then you better catch up on your French, and we will put you with the other girl again."

"Fine, I'll stay with Emmaline."

"You two only have to get along for a day, then you guys won't have to speak to each other anymore. Does that sound like a deal, you two?"

"Deal!" We both shouted at the exact same time.

The rest of the day went okay. Emmaline and I barely spoke to each other. I learned the basics of school. As long as you listen, do you work, and know your place, then you will do fine while being here. I enjoyed most of my classes. Especially my dance class. This was the last class of my day. It allowed me to get all my anger and frustrations out. They were doing a famous dance that I already did in California. At the end of class, the teacher came up and talked to me.

"Ms. Liliana, what you showed us in class was amazing. We only started practicing this piece the other day, and you already have it down perfectly. How is that possible?"

"First, may you please call me, Lily? I don't like Liliana. Thank you, Mrs. Nitch. Second, I already did this dance at my old school in California. I actually helped a lot of my friends with this, my teacher wanted me to help the class."

"I will start calling you by Lily, thank you for correcting me. I can't believe you managed to teach others this dance. This is a hard dance. Would you be willing to help me with students here?"

"Sure, I'll help."

"Thank you, Lily."

"It's no problem. I love seeing other people succeed."

When I got home, my parents were on the couch putting more furniture together. I ran up to them and did the unspeakable. I knew when my parents were focused on something, they hated being interrupted. They wanted to keep their minds on the task in front of them. I grabbed everything from their hands and started jumping up and down to get their attention.

"Mom, Dad, you guys won't believe how today went!"

"Ho..."

"My day went amazingly! It first started out terrible by some girls making fun of me. I ignored them though. After, since you said I could speak and understand French, I had to wait for the principal to change my schedule, but it gave me some time to relax, and play on my tablet. I did get in an argument, but it made me realize that not everyone is going to like me. I have to accept the fact and live life to the fullest. Dance class was last, so all of the bad things of the day were worth the wait. My dance teacher admired my dancing, I did the dance perfectly. I learned the dance before leaving San Diego. My teacher asked if I would help her teach the class, so the other students could learn from me. I obviously said I would. I am happy. Thank you guys for making me move here, and making me realize there is good that can come out of this situation. I love you guys!"

"You're welcome, Lily. We are glad you enjoyed your first day. The news about dancing is fantastic! We told you that you would be fine with your dancing career. Now, can we please get back to putting furniture together? We would love to have a dinner table and dressers."

"Yes, sorry. I am extremely joyful and couldn't hold the news any longer. I am going to do some homework before dinner."

I ran up to my room, played some music, and got to work. I knew this change was going to be a good one. I eventually fell asleep while doing homework. When my parents came to check on me, I had my laptop opened to an essay I was writing, and my completed homework beside me. My dad had to pick me up and carry me over to my bed since I was at my computer stand. The only reason I knew my parents checked on me was that when I woke up in the middle of the night, I was in my bed. I guess I was too excited to go back to school.

Chapter 4

The next day at school, as soon as I walked into the building, I saw Emmaline. She got in my face, and started yelling, "You stupid new girl who thinks she knows everything! You will never be better than me!" As she continued to yell, she proceeded to push me down and punch me in the face. Instead of getting up and fighting back, I got up and continued to class. Most of my teachers didn't seem to notice I had a black eye, or my nose was bleeding. The only teacher who truly seemed to care was my dance teacher. Right when I walked into class, she pulled me into the hallway to have a conversation with me.

"What in the world happened, Lily? You look terrible."

"It's nothing. I fell and hit my face on a locker. I will be alright. I promise."

"Stop lying to me, Lily. I know you didn't fall. Now tell me the truth."

"Okay, fine. Emmaline got mad at me because she thinks I am better than her, so she beat me up. Nobody else has noticed, or if they did, never asked me about it. I didn't want to tell on Emmaline. I was afraid of what would happen next if I told."

"Don't ever be afraid, Lily. I will take care of it. Right now, you will be going to see the nurse, so you can get all cleaned up. Don't worry about class today. Take care of yourself. Remember, you are special and unique. No one can take that title away from you. I will always be here for you, no matter what happens in life."

"Thank you."

When I was walking to the nurse's office, I ran into Emmaline. My hands started shaking and I started sweating furiously. I kept my head held high while trying to ignore her evil stare. Even though I kept staring straight, I couldn't avoid her. When I walked past her, she held her foot up and tried to trip me. When I fell, I hit my head on the ground. It started throbbing. I got all dizzy and couldn't see correctly. Luckily, I was only a few feet away from the nurse's office. When I went in there, I had to wait a few minutes. I could barely keep my eyes open, but I forced myself to stay awake. I didn't want anything to happen if I did damage something. The task of staying awake was extremely difficult. As soon as the nurse walked in, I fainted and fell to the ground. The nurse called for backup and called for an ambulance. Everything was a fuzz afterward and I barely remember anything. All I know is when I woke up, I was surrounded by a lot of people in a hospital room.

When I first opened my eyes, I saw people in my room, but I couldn't remember who they were for the life of me. There was a guy on my left, who was my dad. My mom was on my right. My dance teacher and my sister were in the room too. Even though I now know who they were, they were complete strangers at the time. My head was killing me and my mom was trying to have a simple conversation with me.

"Lily, can you hear me?"

"I can hear you, but I have a question. Who are you?"

When my mom heard the question, she called the nurses in and they took me into an emergency CT scan to see why I couldn't remember who anyone was. Everything again was a rush, the CT scan showed no signs of bleeding or swelling, and the exam revealed I had suffered from short term memory loss and a concussion. The doctors said recovery for both things could take up to three months at the earliest, and sometimes over a year. They said the treatment for both was to take it easy, and no dancing for at least six months, or until I have gotten cleared by a doctor. I had to stay in the hospital overnight, so I could be observed. If I showed any other symptoms of my concussion getting worse, they would treat it right away. I had a hard time falling asleep at night. Also, when I was sleeping, I kept tossing and turning. I kept having a dream about everything. When I kept having my flashbacks, though, I remember waking up whenever the part of Emmaline punching me to the ground came around. I wanted to go back in time and change how everything happened.

The next day, I got told I was allowed to go home. For school, I was only allowed to go for half a day, and dance was out of the question. At that point, I still didn't understand how serious my injuries were, and still tried to dance. When my parents caught me dancing, they would grab me and make me sit on the couch, afraid of dizzy spells. This went on for the next month. I eventually was able to start reading again. Reading was the one thing besides dancing I missed the most.

One day at school, my dance teacher came to me right before I had to leave, and gave me a note. It was a long one too.

Lily. I am first going to apologize for such a long letter. I know this may be hard for you to read, but I needed to let you know of something important you may like to know. The day you got injured, I received the news of you getting hurt even more which caused you to get sent to the hospital. After class, the police came to me and questioned me about everything I knew, or may have heard. I told them you came to class already injured, and I sent you to get checked out by the nurse. I told them you said Emmaline beat you up. They said they would check into it. When they went to question her, she said she didn't put a finger on you. I personally don't believe her. Both herself and her brother are troublemakers and have had several problems before. The police said when you were awake, they would come and talk to you. The only problem was the hospital wouldn't allow them. Questioning you wouldn't be helpful since you couldn't remember anything. A couple of days later, they said since there was no evidence of anyone actually hurting you, they were going to close the case. When I heard those words come out of the investigator's mouth, all I wanted to do was yell and say they didn't know anything and how much pain you were in.

I got a text message the same night. Attached to it was a video. Someone caught Emmaline beating you up. The person who sent me the video wants to stay anonymous, so I am not allowed to tell you who was watching. The next day, I went in after school to the investigators so they could see the video. After seeing the footage, they went to Emmaline's house and arrested her. She is in jail for thirty days and two hundred hours of community service with assault charges against her. This is why she hasn't been to school. I don't know if you have noticed or not because of your memory, but I that it would be good for you to know. They will be checking the cameras again to see if anything else has happened. I know you won't be able to dance for a while, but this summer I would like for you to be a dance counselor for a group of ten girls whose ages range from five to ten. If you are able to, I would love to have you for this position. I think you would make a great candidate for it.

Remember, you are special and no one can take that away from you.

After reading the note, my face got red and a smile came across my face. It was a smile I hadn't had on my face for the last month. I did have a little remorse though about Emmaline being in jail, but after thinking about it, she deserved it. She deserved everything she got after this. She had to get through that big pretty head of hers, she isn't going to be the best at everything she does. There are going to be people like me, who are naturally good at things and maybe better than her. I definitely had a lot to think about with this summer dance camp. I wanted to do it, but I don't think I would be any better by the time I had to start. It was already December, and the camp started in June. The doctors said there was a chance I wouldn't be better until next November. It was something I needed to pray for.

The following week was Christmas. I was super pumped for Christmas, it brought back memories which I look back on and they make me joyful. One memory was last year when I was performing in a dance recital. It was my first time proving to my parents I wanted to dance for a living. I remember I was on stage, I had to do this difficult ballet move. It required me to do four spins and jump over someone on the other side of the stage. I almost messed up doing it, but the other person I was supposed to jump over helped me out by moving closer to me, so I could make it over them. I made the landing perfectly while everybody stood up to give me a round of applause. I was proud of myself.

While thinking about it, I was starting to believe it was the last recital I would be a part of for a long while. I wasn't sure I even wanted to continue. I didn't want to run into anyone else who thought I was better than them, and I didn't want to get any more unexpected injuries because of jealousy.

Besides the memories, I loved decorating for Christmas. All the baking, playing Christmas music, and last but not least, all the gifts. Now, I didn't necessarily like receiving gifts, but I love buying them, wrapping each individual gift, laying them under the tree, or personally delivering them. I used to love receiving gifts when I was little, but one Christmas Eve when I was seven, my perspective got changed for the better, I believe.

Chapter 5

At that age, my parents took me to a homeless shelter to help serve Christmas dinner. When we first got there the people looked all cold and scared. I didn't understand why, until my dad told me the people we were serving either lived on the streets or had to stay in a homeless shelter. This was why a lot of these people didn't look the way we did. They weren't fortunate enough to have the luxuries we did. While I was serving food, some of the people looked at me like I was crazy. Some people started a conversation with me. I had the opportunity to tell about my life with dancing. They were interested in knowing more, so the people who wanted to listen to me actually did. They left me with encouraging words which made me believe I could actually dance.

I am still in contact with some of those people today. The one lady is actually my pen pal. We write to each other every week. I am waiting for her letter this week. I love Mrs. Marine. It wasn't until a couple of days before Christmas that I got her letter. When I opened it, I couldn't help but cry. This is what it said;

Sweet Lily.

I hope you are having a wonderful Christmas holiday. I am sorry this letter is a little late, but I have some news to tell you. Right before Thanksgiving, I was admitted into the hospital here in San Diego. I was having some stomach problems, so I came to get it checked out. Well, here to find out, I was in one of the last stages of liver cancer. They only give me about three more weeks to live. I get weaker and weaker every day. It is even hard to write this letter, but I knew it had to be done. You will hopefully be getting another letter from my sister here in the next couple of weeks, it will contain something important inside.

I loved being your pen pal and growing with you to see how far you have come from the first time we have met. I hope you understand and don't worry too much about me. We will see each other again in Heaven. I will always remember when you first told me you were a Christian. I was proud to see and hear about a girl like you had so much faith in God.

I love you, sweetie. Don't ever forget it. This isn't a goodbye but a see you later.

P.S. Miss. Dancer.

After I read it I couldn't help but shed a tear or two in front of my parents. They tried to comfort me and ask me what was wrong, but I just pushed them aside and ran up to my room. The one thing that really hit home was when she called me Miss. Dancer. She gave me the name when I sent her a recording of me dancing to her favorite song. The song was Jingle Bell Rock. I had to listen to it one last time so I could remember her. I turned the volume on high.

When my mom came to try and talk to me, she realized what was wrong before she even came into my room. My mom knew when I was listening to Jingle Bell Rock I was thinking of Mrs. Marine. Apparently, my mom knew Mrs. Marine was in the condition that she was in. Both she and Dad did. They didn't want to tell me because they knew I would react this way. I don't blame them, I just wished I had a way to go and say goodbye to Mrs. Marine before she passed away.

When I went to bed, the letter kept running through my head. It took me about three hours to fall asleep. I had to cry myself to sleep. It was a rough night.

When I got up in the morning, there was something underneath my pillow. It was an envelope with my name on it. It was from my parents. Attached to the envelope was another note.

Lily, we know how heartbroken you are about Mrs. Marine. We are truly sorry we didn't tell you about her sooner. We wanted her to tell you herself. There is something inside this envelope we think you may enjoy. We love you, sweetie.

When I opened the envelope, there was a ticket to go back to San Diego to see Mrs. Marine before she passed. When I had the ticket in my hand, I ran down to my parents and gave them the biggest hug of their lives.

"Lily." They were gasping for air and their faces turned red. "Why are you this happy?"

"Thank you guys for the plane ticket. I love you guys!"

"You're welcome, Lily. Now go get ready. Your plane leaves in four hours and we have to be at the airport in an hour and a half."

I sped up the stairs to pack my bag. I was able to stay for a week, this way I could also spend time with Amiah. She didn't know I was coming but her parents did. I was excited, but at the same time, I was sad due to the reason I was going back to San Diego. I was just glad I would hopefully be able to say goodbye to Mrs. Marine one last time. I got done packing in less than ten minutes. I decided to pass time before I left by practicing my dance to Jingle Bell Rock. My one mission when I saw Mrs. Marine was to show her the dance to her favorite song one last time. It always brought a smile to her face when she saw me dancing.

It was time to head to the airport after finishing the dance for the third time. My mom had to take me because my dad got called into work early. I kissed him goodbye and I was off. The feeling of being away from my parents for more than just

43

a couple of hours was nerve-wracking, but I was ready. I am glad they trusted me. The airport was super busy when we got there. Everyone was heading back home after the holidays. It was so crowded. Being the tiny girl I am, I had to push through the crowd and security. In my opinion, it was insane.

It took about two hours for me to go through security and secure my bags. I had to say goodbye to my mom before security. I gave her a kiss and waved goodbye, as I ran to my gate because they said my flight was going to take off in ten minutes. I got on the plane and had a hard time finding my seat because the plane was just as crowded as the airport itself. I was amazed no one had the seat beside me. The trip took about fourteen hours. I had one connection in Texas. During both flights, I continued to think of Mrs. Marine, and if I was going to make it on time or not. I eventually did fall asleep. Sleeping made the time go a lot faster.

At about midnight, my plane finally landed in San Diego. I was well-rested, and when I walked into the airport, I had the most wonderful greeting of all times. Amiah came running up to me yelling like a little girl. My feet came off the ground, and both of us fell to the ground not letting go of each other. We were trying to catch our breath, but it all led to us laughing harder at ourselves. At that moment, I totally forgot about the main reason I came back to San Diego. That is one thing Amiah could do. She could easily make me forget about anything bad happening in my life at the time. I was lucky I had her as a friend.

"I've missed you so much, Lily. My mom thought she could keep the secret from me. The plan backfired on her when you texted her saying you were about to get on your last flight. I had her phone when the text came through. I could barely hold any of my excitement afterward. People started looking at me when we walked through the airport because I kept saying, 'Lily is coming. Lily is coming. I can't wait!' I also may or may not have been jumping up and down like a psychopath."

"Seems like you, Amiah. I am glad to be back for a few days. First thing tomorrow though, I am heading up to the hospital. I need to say my last goodbyes."

"Okay, Lily. I am sorry you have to go through all of this. I know how much Mrs. Marine means to you. She will always hold a special place in your heart, I know."

"Yes, she will. Can we go back to your house so I can get settled in?"

"Yes, we can."

On the way back to Amiah's house, it gave us a chance to catch up and tell each other all the gossip that was happening in our parts of the world. I allowed her to go first because she seemed much more excited to tell me about things than I was to tell her all the bad things that had happened to me.

She told me about Mike, the guy I used to like. He asked the one cheerleader out to homecoming in front of the whole school, and he got embarrassed because she turned him down in front of more than two thousand kids. I couldn't believe what I was hearing. No one had ever had the nerve to turn Mike down. He was the captain of the football team and always seemed to get his way, even when he got in trouble.

Amiah told the story about how Mike and another football player got into an argument and into a physical fight. Mike beat the crap out of the other dude. He was supposed to get suspended from school for a week and be off the team for the rest of the season. This incident happened right before the school was supposed to go to playoffs, and Mike was one of

45

their best players. Of course, his dad paid for his son to get off the suspension of at least the team, so Mike could help get the team to the State championship. The school hadn't gone to States in the past fifteen years, so that was the one year they actually had a chance, but they needed their star player to achieve the goal. He did lead the team to States and even won them. I was impressed. After Amiah was done telling her story, we were already at her place. I promised her before we went to bed, I would tell her everything which had been happening to me since we last talked.

I got all my stuff unpacked, and went to get a shower. Little did I know, Amiah's older brother Andrew was home. I thought he moved in with his girlfriend and her parents right before I left. Well, that relationship didn't last long. The only issue with this was when I went to go get a shower, I wasn't expecting anyone to be in the bathroom, but Andrew was, so I accidentally walked in on him. He was totally naked but quickly covered up. I covered my eyes and went back into the bedroom.

"Amiah! You didn't tell me Andrew was back home. I just walked in on him in the bathroom. It was not a sight I wanted to see."

"Sorry, Lily. I did not realize he was in the bathroom. He is usually in bed by this time. It was my mistake. I should have let you know either way."

"It's okay, Amiah."

When Andrew walked out of the bathroom, he was clothed and came to apologize.

"I'm sorry, Lily. I was planning on already being done by the time you guys got home, but I fell asleep after they left, so I just got in the shower a few minutes ago."

"It's okay, Andrew. I didn't realize you were back home. If I did, I would have knocked before entering. Lesson learned: knock on any door in the house before entering."

We all three started cracking up. I eventually did get in the shower.

When I was done, I got all ready for bed, and right when I was about to fall asleep Amiah came running over to me, shaking me and yelling at me to tell her everything which had been happening in my life ever since I left San Diego.

"I'm tired, Amiah. Can it wait until tomorrow?"

"You promised, Lily."

"Okay. Well, here it goes. When I started my new school there was this one girl who was totally jealous of me. It got to the point where she beat me up, and in the process, she gave me a black eye, a broken nose, and a concussion. The concussion is making me not be allowed to do dance for at least two more months, but could possibly be up to a year. I still get headaches every once in a while, but so far I think I am getting better."

"This is insane, Lily. How can anyone be jealous of you? You are absolutely amazing."

"That's the problem, Amiah. I need to be a little less amazing."

When I said that, I started laughing harder than I had before. I fell off the bed and banged my head. Amiah came rushing over to me making sure I was okay.

"Lily! Are you okay? Say something to me, please!"

"I'm okay, Amiah. I told you, I am getting better. Now let's go to bed. I have a long day tomorrow, and I don't know what you and your family have planned."

"Okay, Lily."

It took us a couple of minutes to fall asleep, due to the fact we kept laughing and couldn't stop. The flight got in at midnight, and so it was a quarter past one when I finally fell asleep. I had an amazing night's sleep, knowing I was where I belonged. I didn't want to go back to Paris. I wanted to stay with my best friend and her family. I knew it wasn't going to happen, but a girl can always dream.

The next morning, I was the first one up and ready. I wanted to get to the hospital as soon as I possibly could. I left at about seven-thirty in the morning. The hospital was only about five minutes away from Amiah's house, so I walked instead of getting anyone up and asking for a ride. It was a cold but pretty winter morning. This was another thing I missed about San Diego. I missed the wind blowing in my face and making me remember being a kid again. I took in the fresh air, and took one step in front of the other, trying to prepare myself for what I was about to see when I walked into the hospital room. I finally got to my destination. I slowly walked up to the front desk and asked where Mrs. Marine was. They told me she was in room two-twenty. When they said that number, I couldn't help but bring a smile to my face. Two twenty is the time when I first met Mrs. Marine. It is our lucky number. I slowly opened the door, and right in front of me was Mrs. Marine all hooked up to machines. She was sitting up and smiling. I took it as a good sign. I went and grabbed her hand.

"Mrs. Marine. How are you today? Do you know who I am?"

She smiled the contagious smile she had. "Lily." Her voice was quiet and weak. I was glad she knew who I was, but it broke my heart seeing how bad she was getting.

"Yes, Mrs. Marine, it's me, Lily. How are you?"

"I'm good but my time is coming to an end."

"I know, Mrs. Marine. I wanted to come and say goodbye, and show you one last thing."

I took out my phone and put Jingle Bell Rock on. I started dancing and the smile on Mrs. Marine's face got gigantic. I was in the middle of the song when all of a sudden Mrs. Marine started breathing extremely hard. I stopped in the middle of my tracks and ran over to her.

"Are you okay, Mrs. Marine? Speak to me, please! Don't leave me! I need you here!"

Mrs. Marine handed me an envelope. "Lily, I love you. This isn't goodbye." Those were her last words. She passed right there in my arms. I started crying, and the alarms from the machines made all the nurses come in. They gently took me out of the room so they could take care of everything since Mrs. Marine was no longer with us. I opened the envelope she gave me.

Lily.

If you are reading this letter it means I am no longer living here on Earth, but I am living with our Lord in Heaven. This letter is going to tell you everything from what I have been feeling to my last thoughts. From the first moment we met, I knew you were a special girl, who could achieve anything you put your mind to. I was always excited to see you dance, and hear about everything God was doing in your life. You had this way of making me smile whenever you walked through the room. I told everyone about you and your passion for dancing. You kept my life interesting and made me believe there was still some good in the world.

The biggest thing I wanted to tell you though, is one person I told about your dancing is a dance teacher at Juilliard in New York City. The school you have always dreamed about going to. I might or might not have sent her a video of you dancing, and she replied back saying she was really interested in having you as a student. You would have to wait until you were done with high school though. She said, as soon as you were done with high school she would get a hold of you, and talk to you more in-depth about the school, and the possibility of having you as a dance student there for at least a year.

I love you, Lily, and always will, even when I'm not down here on Earth. I will be your guardian angel. You may have times when you want to give up, but I will be right there. All you have to do is call out my name, and you will know for sure I am with you. Now, I will be on your journey as you follow your dreams. I can't wait to see who you become.

Now, go and live your life, Miss. Dancer. Always remember, two-twenty.

After reading the note, I couldn't help but have a rainfall of tears come down my face. I loved Mrs. Marine and couldn't believe or take in she was gone. I knew she was right there beside me along my journey.

The next couple of days were a blur. I went to her calling hours and funeral. Every part of it was extravagant, but depressing at the same time. I knew none of her family but they all knew who I was. When she said she told everyone about me, she wasn't joking. At the end of the funeral, her sister asked me if I would like to dance for them one last time in remembrance of Mrs. Marine. Of course I said yes. There was no better way for me to express how much Mrs. Marine meant to me than for me to dance for everyone.

When I started dancing, there was total silence in the room. No one spoke a word during the whole duration of the dance, but at the end of the dance, there was not a single dry eye in the room. I couldn't believe everyone liked my dancing. I was still a little hesitant since I wasn't allowed dancing because of my concussion, but I couldn't give the chance to dance for one special person up. I did start getting a headache afterward, but I took my medicine and felt better right away.

The same night, I had to catch a plane back home. The trip went slower than the trip there, but it gave me time to reflect on the last couple of days. Whether I wanted to admit or not, I was ready to go home.

Chapter 6

When I got back to Paris, both of my parents were there to comfort me. Amiah's mom called them the other day and updated them on what happened.

"We are sorry, Lily, to hear about Mrs. Marine. We know how much she meant to you."

"It's okay. Life happens and we have to move on from it. She is now my guardian angel and is with me every step of the way."

"Yes, she is, Lily. We are always here as well if you ever want to talk about anything."

"Thank you, Mom and Dad. Can we go get something to eat? I am starving."

"You read our minds. We were planning on going to grab a bite to eat, once we got back into town. Do you want to go to the restaurant we first went to when we arrived in Paris? We know how much you enjoyed eating there."

"Yes, please."

"Okay. We will go there then."

As we were on our way to the restaurant, I stayed quiet most of the time. I'm not usually the observing kind of person, but tonight seemed to be different. I observed everything from how the ground laid, to how tall the trees were, and how the clouds seemed to go into different formations. I noticed the one cloud looked like a dance trophy, the one Mrs. Marine gave me since she thought I deserved one, even after I messed up at a recital. I still have the trophy sitting on my desk at home. It is the first thing I see when I wake up in the morning.

Right at that moment, I felt at peace. I knew everything would fall into place right when it needed to.

When we got to the restaurant, I ordered my favorite plate. It was this French bread with bacon and sausage on it. I licked my lips together as the waitress was bringing out the food. I could already taste it without it in front of me yet. During dinner, my parents and I laughed and told stories. They got me to be myself. I had to admit, I was having an amazing time, and was glad to be back with people who I knew loved me. The rest of the night went slowly, but it was a good night, even if I was tired from the plane ride. All I wanted was everything to go back to normal, and not even have to think about the passing of Mrs. Marine.

The next morning, I went back to school. The first person I saw when I walked through the doors was Emmaline. I got scared for my life and ran to the dance room hoping my dance teacher was there. I didn't think Emmaline was supposed to be out of jail yet, but then again she had served a month in jail. When I got to the room, I looked all around for Mrs. Nitch but she was nowhere to be found. My heart started pounding faster, I was losing my breath, and I was getting dizzy. I couldn't take the chance of Emmaline seeing me. I was still recovering from the concussion she gave me a month ago. I started crying when the thought came across my mind. When Mrs. Nitch came into the room, she found me standing in the middle of the dance floor in a daze.

"Lily. Are you okay? What is going on?"

"Emma…" My face started getting red, and I couldn't even finish a simple sentence.

"Lily. What are you trying to say? I can't understand you when you are crying this badly." Mrs. Nitch sat me down, and let me calm down a few minutes before trying to talk to me again. "Now, Lily. What is wrong?"

"I saw Emmaline."

"Oh, Lily. I was hoping I would have time to tell you before you found out this way."

"Before I found out what?"

"Sit down. The investigators looked over the video I had in my possession and went to question Emmaline again. She still thought she could get away with everything and lied again, but they showed her the video, she flipped out and threatened to come to kill you. She wanted to make sure you didn't have a chance to ever dance again. The police then took her into custody, and are moving her into a big prison. The police, who didn't want to make a huge deal of the situation, dressed in regular old street clothes so they could escort her to the school so she could get her stuff. Her parents wanted her stuff back, but they couldn't come get it. Mr. Frankford told her she could come into school today before anyone else to get all of her stuff. She obviously won't be coming back, she also lost her whole scholarship to the school. She lives in rural France, not in Paris, so the only reason she was able to come to school is because of a dance scholarship. Well, she ruined her chance when she beat you up. She was supposed to be out by the time you got here, but I forgot you sometimes you come in before school to get help with school work, since you only come in for half a day anyway, due to your concussion.

"You will be fine, Lily. You have nothing to worry about. How about this? I'll make you a deal. I'll walk with you to your first class, so if she isn't out of school yet, you will have protection, and she won't be able to lay a hand on you. How does that sound?"

"I love your idea, Mrs. Nitch. Thank you."

"You're welcome, Lily. Like I told you before, I will always make sure you are safe."

"I appreciate it a lot."

Walking down the halls before school hours felt weird to me. I didn't know why though, I had been doing it for a little more than a month. Maybe it was just because I knew Emmaline was out of jail, but then again she was supposed to be going to prison today. I didn't realize assaulting someone to the point they got a concussion could send you to prison. I mean it's bad, but I didn't think it was as serious as they made it sound.

I luckily got to my first class of the day with no sight of Emmaline. Maybe the time has come to where she had to go and turn herself into prison. The feeling gave me some comfort, but at the same time, I felt really bad she had to go to prison.

There was something else I couldn't figure out. Who recorded Emmaline beating me up and took the video to Mrs. Nitch? I wanted to know, so I could thank them. Also, maybe they knew something I didn't know about Emmaline, and the situation she got herself into.

For the next couple of days, I was very observant of my surroundings. Maybe the person I was looking for would follow me around and I would catch them. All it took was me watching and making sure I took into account everything I did on the day of the incident.

As the next few days went past, I didn't catch a lead on who I was looking for. I didn't know if it had anything to do with me not being good at remembering anything, or me not watching carefully. I even asked Mrs. Nitch if she remembered anyone I interacted with, but she said she couldn't remember anything after she told me to go see the nurse. I got so wrapped up with investigating, my school work started getting behind. When I didn't want to admit to my parents the things I was doing, I blamed it on my concussion.

My parents thought it would be best to take me back to the hospital to see if it was really my concussion. When we got to the hospital, they gave me another CT scan to see if they could find anything different around my brain. I must have either thought I was funny, or I was totally out of it because the doctors told my parents the first thing I said when I got back into the scan room was, "you aren't going to find anything in my brain because I just so happen not to have a brain." The doctors got a pretty good laugh out of it. I can't remember why I said it, but I did.

After I came out of the scanner, the doctors told my parents they couldn't find anything different, but they did think I was healing faster than they thought I would. They were discussing the idea of in a month or so, I could gradually start doing dance again. When I heard the news, I sprang up and started jumping up and down like a little kid. The doctors had to literally grab me and set me back down on a chair, and hold me down. I had to promise I would stay calm.

"Now, Lily. We say this, but it isn't a promise you will be able to start dance in a month. It is just a general thought. We will have you come back for a check-up before we give you a definite answer."

"I understand. I have faith my check-up will be good, and you will be able to tell me I am able to start dancing again. I don't want this injury to define how I live the rest of my life. I have big dreams, and I am not going to let a stupid injury get in my way of achieving those dreams."

"We are glad you have a positive outlook on this, but we don't want you to get your hopes up if you can't dance in a month."

"I won't get my hopes up, just being positive."

"Good."

After my check-up, the hospital sent me home since they couldn't find anything wrong. They suggested I rest and take the next day off school, in case I was starting to develop a further brain injury. Even though I liked school, I wanted to take the day off and take the time to understand I was safe, and Emmaline couldn't hurt me anymore since she was going to be locked up for a long while.

That night, I fell asleep right away. I was surprised, since lately I haven't been able to sleep because of my head, or I would feel sick and be afraid to fall asleep. Maybe it was because I was thinking about finally being able to dance again, or knowing Emmaline couldn't attack me anymore. I had what started as a peaceful dream.

It was when I stepped on the stage for the first time after my concussion was cleared. I was the only one on stage though. There were no other dancers, which was weird because I always dance with other people; even if I had a solo dance, there were still other dancers on stage with me. I ignored the fact and continued with the routine I had spent hours preparing. There were over a thousand people in the audience wanting to watch me. My heart was beating fast just like it would if I ran a marathon. I didn't think I could do the dance by myself. I never had to dance by myself. I decided to go on with the performance.

I froze in the middle of it because I had a feeling something wasn't right. I was correct. When I was a minute and a half from the end of my routine, the door to the theater was knocked down, and there was a skinny bald guy that came rushing in and shooting. He first aimed at the people in the crowd, and then he came shooting at me. When he shot at me, he missed, but I pretended I had been shot so he didn't continue. As soon as I hit the ground, I woke up from the terrible nightmare, screaming my head off. It sounded like I was actually getting murdered or seriously injured. My parents came running in.

"What the heck is going on, Lily?"

"I had a dream that started out amazing but ended in a horrible nightmare. I dreamt about myself and other people getting shot at one of my recitals."

"You want to rest and relax, so in a month you can dance again. It was only a dream."

"Yeah, maybe you guys are right. I think I am just stressed because I am wanting to dance again, and can imagine how I will be feeling if I get the okay to be back on stage."

"We understand, Lily. Now get some rest. Goodnight." Both my mom and dad gave me a kiss on the forehead.

It took me about another hour to fall asleep again. I didn't want to have the same dream again, even though I knew it was my mind playing games on me, and making me think I wouldn't get better. When I did fall back to sleep, I slept peacefully. I think I slept for another six hours.

When I got up, I ate breakfast and tried to do some homework so I didn't get behind in school more than I already was. The day went smoothly. My mom stayed home from work to help me and make sure my behavior didn't change, and if it did, someone would be there to take me to the hospital right away. I felt fine other than a headache, which I always got ever since my concussion happened. Around four o'clock there was a knock on the door. My mom was sleeping since she didn't get much sleep the night before. I usually wasn't allowed to answer the door unless my mom or dad was awake and with me, but when I looked through the peephole I recognized who it was. It was Mrs. Nitch. I didn't understand why she was at my door. I thought she would have still been at school. When I answered the door, Mrs. Nitch gave me a letter, and said she couldn't stay but hoped I would like what the letter said.

Lily.

I know you are having hopes you are going to start dancing again in a month. Well, I wanted to give you some news, but I didn't know when to tell you just in case you didn't heal like you were expecting to. There is a college dance teacher in New York City that is looking to recruit you next year, once you graduate high school. You would be the youngest student in her class since she only deals with Juniors and Seniors in college, but she has seen you dance and wants you in her class. I have told her great things about you. I have faith that you will be able to heal completely and go show Mrs. Bean what you were born to do. You need to show the world you can do whatever you set your mind to, no matter what obstacles you have to go through. I hope this letter helped get you caught up on what you should be looking forward to when you get better.

I love you, Lily, and I will see you when you come back to school.

After reading the letter from Mrs. Nitch, I wanted to get better right away. I couldn't let Mrs. Bean down. It would be a dream come true if I could dance with Juniors and Seniors in college as a Freshman.

As the next couple of hours went by all I did was rest and didn't even try to get up and dance. I knew rest was the only thing that could help my concussion. I started to feel much better after a couple of days of rest.

After a week, I started to do more school and a little bit more of dance, but just enough to make sure I didn't make my concussion worse.

The next few days went slowly when I needed them to go fast because I wanted Friday to come around, so I could see if I could start dance once again. I did try to sneak some dancing in, but every time I did my parents would yell at me to stop. Friday did finally come around. In the morning, I got up, ate breakfast, did some homework and got ready to go back to the hospital. I was extremely anxious and wanted to know the results.

Once we got to the hospital, it took them forty minutes to get me in because there were so many people. Once I got back to the room, they took me to do some more tests. As I was laying on the table, the nurse must have seen I was nervous, since my hands were trembling. They had to do another CT scan on my brain after the first one just to make sure they caught everything they needed to. She came over to me, and as she put her hand on my shoulder, she said; "It is going to be okay, Lily, whatever the outcome is. I know you are nervous, but you need to relax so we can get a better CT scan."

As the nurse kept her hand on my shoulder and kept me calm, the male tech took the rest of the scans. After the CT scans were completed, I had to go back to the room to wait for the results. When I got into the room, I started to talk to my mom and dad about the letter Mrs. Nitch gave me again. In the middle of me talking, the doctor came in with a smile on her face. I knew what the face meant, but instead of getting ahead of myself, I waited patiently for her to tell me.

"Lily. I have some good news for you."

"What is it?"

"The CT scan came back clear, and you now have the doctors okay to start dancing again, but still take it easy for the next week and a half."

After I heard the news, I jumped out of my seat and started jumping up and down like a little girl who just got candy. My excitement got ahead of myself. I hugged the doctor and my parents. I couldn't wait until Monday so I could go back to school and start dancing again.

Chapter 7

When I got back to school on Monday, we all started to learn a new dance. Apparently, when I missed a couple of days of school, the principal decided she wanted the dance team to put on a Spring performance for the whole school. Mrs. Nitch thought it was a good idea, but it was the wrong timing. Especially since we were having a lot of competitions coming up, so recruiters from different schools could come and watch to see if they wanted any of us to come and dance at their school. I didn't have to worry about being recruited since I was basically already recruited, but instead of going to a big fancy school right away, I was going straight to the Varsity dance team when I entered college in the fall.

Mrs. Nitch did have a concern about me doing the Spring performance because she didn't want me to take the chance and hurt myself or anyone else before I had the chance to fully recover, and be able to participate in the Varsity team. I wanted to agree with her, but I also wanted to do the Spring performance. After a couple of days of conversation, I reluctantly agreed to not participate in the Spring performance. The only good side of me not performing was Mrs. Nitch put me in charge of all the choreography. In my opinion, putting together choreography was even harder than dancing, because you had to teach all the girls what to do and where to do it in the music. Where if I was dancing, I would just have to go through the dance once watching someone do it and then usually I would be able to do the whole thing by myself. That in itself showed my dance teacher and my parents dancing came to me easily, and I was a natural at it. I spent hours at home after practice coming up with the perfect dance moves, which went along with the music we were doing. When I was practicing, I felt like I was truly practicing to perform at the Spring performance.

I knew it wasn't real though, because when the day the actual performance came, Mrs. Nitch would not allow me to step foot on the stage, instead she would make me sit in the front row of the audience and record the whole thing. This was Mrs. Nitch's thing, whenever we had a performance she or someone else would videotape the performance, and the next day in class we would watch the tape and watch for the things we could improve on for the next performance.

The night came that I was dreading because I still had to get ready with all the girls which made me even angrier because I wasn't able to dance with them and give the audience a performance that was going to blow their minds. I had faith in the girls though, and I was confident in myself that I did well with teaching the girls the dance moves that they needed to make their performance the best that it could be.

Right before the program was supposed to start though something terrible happened. My friend Amanda got sick and couldn't dance. I couldn't believe it. Now even though this was a bad thing for the dance it was a good thing for me. I was taking this as my sign that I needed to dance. I didn't say anything to Mrs. Nitch because I wanted her to come to me and she did just that.

"Lily, you need to dance to take Amanda's part. She cannot dance if she is sick."

"Mrs. Nitch, I can't dance either if I don't want to risk getting hurt again before Mrs. Bean sees me dance."

"Lily, you have to. If you don't dance then we won't have a performance."

All the girls stared me down like I was some kind of mad man. They all started yelling at me, and saying, "Lily, come on please do this for us, You can do it, Lily, you know all the dance moves, Help us out." After hearing all the girls out and seeing the looks on their faces I decided to dance because I couldn't let my friends down. They were more than friends to me at this point. They were a part of my family.

I had to quickly get dressed and my makeup done in less than five minutes. Well, that was wishful thinking because that did not happen. It took twenty minutes for me to get ready and so that resulted in the program starting late and a couple of the people in the audience getting mad at us. When the curtains opened we saw a couple of people leaving the theater. We tried not to get discouraged but that was hard because we worked so hard to try and make tonight perfect, and we didn't want people leaving before we even had a chance to show them what we worked so hard to put together. As soon as the music started things changed.

People looked back right when I took my first step and they all rushed back to their seats to watch the rest of the show. I knew that I was good but I didn't think I was good enough to make people hurry back to their seats to watch what was happening. I was in my happy place. I was being extra cautious to make sure that I wouldn't hurt my ankle again. There was the one dance move in the song 'Love Me Like Never Before' I wasn't sure if I could do, because it would mean that I had to leap in the air and twirl while landing on my bad ankle. I knew I had to do it because that was one of Amanda's biggest solos in the program. All the girls knew that I was having a hard time with the move. When that part came up all of the girls looked towards me to see if I could actually pull it off.

When it came down to thirty seconds before I had to make the move, my hands started to sweat and my face got as red as a tomato. I started to count down in my head ten... nine... eight... seven... six... five... four... three... two... one. I made the move and I landed the ending perfectly. Everyone got up from their seats and started cheering while we finished the rest of the song. At the end of the performance, all of the girls including Amanda ran up to me and gave me a huge group hug. My parents came a few moments after that and gave me a bouquet of flowers.

Although I did like all the attention there was something I had to do. During the performance, I saw Amanda and she looked perfectly fine so I knew something was up. I escaped from the crowd and pulled Amanda to the side.

"Amanda. What is going on? You look perfectly fine to me and don't look anywhere to being sick."

"I am sick, Lily." As Amanda said that she fake coughed.

I smacked Amanda on the shoulder. "Spill it, girly. I know that was a fake cough. Why are you faking being sick? It should have been you up there on that stage dancing your heart out."

"Lily, did you not see yourself up there. You were having a much better time than I would have. You rocked it. That last solo you did was amazing and especially since you landed that ending perfectly. There is no way I would have been able to do what you did up there. Plus I knew how upset you were about not dancing today but having to do everything to prepare for it and so I thought I would give you the chance that you deserved. Everyone came to see you and only you anyways. The only people that came to see the rest of us dance were our parents but there were a lot more people in that audience besides our parents. A lot of people from the community came and they only came to watch you. They have seen you and your sister dance and have fallen in love with you. You are one of the best dancers there are in this school let alone the community. Trust me on this one it was for the best of us that I faked sick and you were the one up on that stage."

"Thanks, Amanda but you didn't have to do that for me. I would have been perfectly okay with sitting in the audience and watching all of you girls. I will admit that I did enjoy dancing but what would have happened if I hurt my ankle again? I can't risk hurting it again before this summer. I have an opportunity to be in dance class with only Junior and Senior college girls next year as long as my ankle feels better.

"I'm waiting to make sure that I can fully dance again. Also, I am trying not to get my hopes up because every time I do then something else goes wrong and I either get hurt or disappointed. Plus it means that I won't be in France."

"Wait, what? The school isn't here in France? Where is it then?"

"No, it isn't here in France. It is in New York City. That is in the United States."

"I know where it is, Lily. I am not stupid. Why would you go to school all the way in the United States?"

"Amanda. The school is a prestigious college there. It is paying me full tuition when I am there. I have to take this opportunity that I am given. I am also from there."

"I can't believe you, Lily. You are leaving all of us here!"

After that Amanda ran off crying. I tried to run after her to explain it but she was a fast runner and I wasn't as fast as I would have liked to be. I couldn't believe that Amanda was acting this way. I thought she would be happy for me. I didn't know what I could do to make it up to her and try to make her feel better about this whole situation. I decided that I would let her go and cool off for a little bit before I went to try and talk to her again.

An hour went by and Amanda still wouldn't talk to me. She must have told all of the other girls about my plan because no one would talk to me or answer any of my texts. I got really upset with everyone. I don't know why everyone was upset with me and couldn't just be happy for me. I knew I was going to do great things in New York City. All I had to do was focus on my dancing and getting better so I could actually go.

A couple of days went by since I told Amanda the news about New York, and she still wouldn't talk to me. That was one of the things that made me make up my mind about accepting the opportunity.

The idea I had was when I was visiting New York to see the city and the new school that I would be dancing a lot of the time. Over the course of the next week, I spent hours coming up with a dance and a plan to go to New York.

At the end of the week, I had the dance down and I had emailed someone at the school to set up a time that I could come to the school so I could do visit. The only problem that occurred with me going to the school is since I'm not eighteen yet and I'm only seventeen, a parent had to come with me or a parent had to fill out papers giving me permission. I guess I didn't think the whole thing out when it came down to it. I knew though that if I got this far then I could come up with a way to get one of my parents to fill out the papers without knowing exactly where I was going. It would most likely be my mom because she was the parent who did things without reading or thinking about what she signed. I knew that my mom signed things without knowing better when she was either extremely tired or first getting out of bed.

My plan was the next morning I would get up extra early, so I could be up before her and when she was getting up, I would ask her to sign the permission slip. I had to make sure that I was already ready though because if I'm ready ahead of time then she would usually goes back to sleep for an extra twenty minutes or so because she wouldn't have to make sure I didn't go back to bed or anything. That was part one of my plan. Part two was going to be more difficult since I had to try and convince my parents to actually let me go to New York to visit this college. My parents had a hard enough time letting me go to California for Mrs. Marine's funeral but they were more willing that time just because I was able to stay with Amiah and her family. We didn't know anyone that lived in New York so I couldn't give them the "well I could stay with this person" card when I went to ask them. I finally did figure out I could tell them that my dance team was going to the school, and then that would back up my reasoning for the permission slip.

That following night, I could barely get any sleep. I was afraid of all the things that could possibly go wrong. Off the top of my head, I could think of three reasons. One, my mom would get up extra early because she couldn't sleep and I wouldn't be able to know to get up even earlier to beat her; two, she would be awake enough to read the permission slip and would find out that it is for a college, or she would have sense and call my dance teacher to make sure that I wasn't lying and make sure that we were actually going to this college for a dance performance. That third scenario was the worst one that could possibly happen out of the three of them. I was really hoping that my plan would work and it wouldn't come to backfire on me. I tried to get all of the bad thoughts out of my head to try and get some sleep so my plan could actually work.

When I finally got to sleep, I kept waking up every hour until finally I said forget it, and stayed up when there was about a half-hour until I had to be up anyway. I got ready and made sure that I had the correct paper for my mom to sign so that way right when she signed it, I could put it in an envelope. When I left for school, I could just quickly put it into the mailbox so it could be sent out today and hopefully the school would get it in the next couple of days.

At five-thirty, I quietly tiptoed into my mother's room and gently shook her arm to wake her up just a little bit.

"What is it, Lily," my mom mumbled under her breath.

"I forgot to have you sign this permission slip for me. Mrs. Nitch is taking the dance class to this school all the way in Chicago, Illinois for a performance by the dance school there. It isn't costing us anything as the college is paying for our transportation and accommodations. Can I go?"

"Yeah, Lily. Bring the paper here so I can go back to sleep since you are already up and ready for school."

"Thank you, Mom. I love you," I gave her a quick hug and kiss and then took the paper and got it ready to be mailed.

I couldn't believe that part of my plan went the way I wanted it to. I was still afraid, though, it was going to go wrong one way or another, but for now, I was just going to focus on it actually working and me getting to New York.

My plan for getting to New York City was as follows. The following Monday, I would get ready for school as planned and leave with all my stuff as if I was going with my class to

New York City. Then, after my mom dropped me off at school I would wait until she left and then catch a cab to the airport and then leave. I knew how to get through the airport by myself since I traveled by plane a lot to get to where I was in my life at that point.

My flight didn't leave until ten-thirty in the morning, so I had about two hours to get to the airport and through security so I could catch my plane on time. The cab came around eight-thirty, and it came right as my mom left the school parking lot. I had to make sure my mom was nowhere in sight before I stepped outside to get into the cab. It was a relaxing ride to the airport. It was about a half-hour away and so I just plugged my headphones into my music and listened to my music for the whole ride there. When we got to the airport the whole cab trip cost me about twenty-seven euros. I was surprised it didn't cost me more. I had the money because I saved the money that I had received as birthday presents and Christmas presents within the past three years. It was hard to find my way through the airport but I did it.

By the time I got through security and everything, it was already ten-fifteen. I had fifteen minutes until my flight left. I went to search for my gate, and as I approached the gate they were boarding. I made it just on time. I couldn't wait to get to this school and see what I was in for in the next year.

Chapter 8

The flight from Paris to New York City was long nine hours. The whole duration of the flight, though, I was planning out how I was really going to get away with this trip, and how I was going to do a music video to show my parents I got an opportunity of a lifetime, to be a student at this prestigious school. I truly wanted to visit the college too, because, from the pictures on the website, it was a beautiful campus, and it was right smack down in the middle of the city. I couldn't wait to spend at least the next year there to make some new friends.

When I got to the airport in New York City, I got lost immediately. The airport was huge. If I were to estimate, there were about three thousand people at the airport. I had to try and find the front of the airport, so I could catch a taxi to the college. The college was only about twenty minutes away. It took me about an hour and a half to finally get to where I needed to go. When I figured out where I was, I had to call the taxi which took about another half hour to get to me. When I got in the taxi, I told the driver I had to go to Juilliard. She knew exactly where it was, and got curious about why a girl like me was going there all by myself. I managed to tell her about my recent incident, and how I recovered much quicker than everybody expected me to. To say the least, she was surprised. We got to Juilliard right when I finished my story. I went to go pay her, and what she did next was out of the ordinary.

"Don't worry about paying, Lily. You have a bright future ahead of you. Think of this as a gift," the young lady said.

"Oh, thank you, but you don't need to pay for me. I don't want you to lose money just because you feel bad for me," I tried to insist on her taking the money.

"Please, Lily. Your story inspired me. I am going through some rough times right now, and I want to do this for you."

"Okay. Thank you. I hope this isn't the last time we will see each other. You are super kind, and I would love to get to know you more."

"I hope not either, Lily. Here take this."

I grabbed the slip of paper she handed me and inside was her number.

"If you are ever back in the city, shoot me a text, and maybe we can catch up and get coffee or dinner."

"I will take you up on the offer. Until next time...Sarah." I closed the door and headed to the front of the school. The school in itself seemed just as big as the airport. It had glass windows so you could see inside, and it had four floors. I couldn't wait to walk in and see what was in store for me.

When I first walked in, I had no idea where to go. There were three halls I could go down, and all three halls seemed like they were endless. I decided to just pick a hall and hope for the best. I first chose the middle hall. As I was walking, there were pictures on the walls of these girls. They had descriptions by them, so I stopped to read some of them. I couldn't stop to read all of them because I had to find where I was supposed to go for this college visit. After about fifteen minutes of wandering, another girl came around and asked me if I needed help.

"Hi. My name is Lily, and I am looking for Mrs. Bean."

The girl must have known exactly who I was talking about because she pointed me down the hall, and to the right where Mrs. Bean's office was.

When I got to where Mrs. Bean was, she was busy on the phone, so she didn't even realize I was there. She had pictures on her wall of what I was guessing of the girls in her class. Under each picture, there was a dancing quote each girl thought was important to her. There was one quote that popped out to me, and it said, "The only dancer you should compare yourself to is the one you used to be." This quote meant a lot to me since my parents had doubts in me when I was younger. I had to be better than who I was the year before, so I could prove to them even though I wasn't like my sister in a lot of ways, I could do what she did, no matter what obstacles came in my way. While I was reading the one quote, I heard, "You must be Lily. The one Mrs. Nitch has been telling me about for the past couple of months."

"Yes. My name is Lily Pene."

"Welcome, Lily. I have heard and seen so much of your dancing, you have blown my mind. I am hoping you will consider coming to Juilliard next year after you graduate. I have already decided to accept you into the dance program if you attend. As you might have heard, I rarely accept Freshman into my dance program. I only take the best of the best, which is usually only Juniors and Seniors."

"Thank you, Mrs. Bean. I am excited to see what this college is like, and hopefully, see myself as a student next year."

"Well, let's get started with this tour. Shall we?"

"We shall."

Mrs. Bean started the tour off by showing me some of the dance rooms I would be spending the majority of my time in. The dance rooms were just like I imagined them to be. They had glass walls all around them. I went to the middle of the one room, and I did a ballet move called the Flying Pas de Chat. I had to jump sideways and while in mid-air, I bend both of my legs up, bringing my feet up as high as possible, with my knees apart. In a Flying Pas de Chat, my first leg is extended. I landed perfectly, and as I did, Mrs. Bean applauded me.

"That was impressive, Lily. I have never seen anyone, not even my dancers I have now, who can do that dance move as perfectly as you did."

"Well, thank you, Mrs. Bean. I have been practicing it for three years now. My sister is the one who helped me perfect move."

"Who is your sister? Does she go here?"

"My sister is Maddy Pene. I don't think she goes here. She left home about four years ago, and I don't see her much anymore."

After I said her name, Mrs. Bean just stood there and froze. "Mrs. Bean?" I waved my hand in front of her to try and get her attention. It took a few moments until she finally came back to reality.

"Maddy Pene is your sister?"

"Yes, ma'am. Is that a problem?"

"No, it's not a problem, except she turned down a full-ride scholarship so she could go to college with her boyfriend at the time. She made a huge mistake. I hope if you decided to come here, you won't be like her."

"I can promise you, Mrs. Bean, if I attend, I will not be like her. I don't focus on boys or being in relationships. I only focus on dance and school."

"Well, I'm glad to hear this. Let's move forward now. I am going to introduce you to some of the girls you will be in class with."

As we continued walking around campus, I saw how beautiful it truly was. Everywhere I looked, there were people walking, smiling, and talking to each other. I didn't see any negativity around at all. I only saw positivity.

We arrived at the one building, and it was a little smaller than the dance studio, but it was still extravagant. When we got into the building it was time for a couple of the classes to dismiss, and everyone was rushing out. I was only five feet and three inches, and a lot of these people were above five feet, five inches. I got trampled by everyone, had to try and catch up with Mrs. Bean, which was hard to do. I had to look up to her, and that in itself was pretty terrifying. I would hate to get on her bad side.

I finally got through the herd of students and saw Mrs. Bean at the end of the hall with another student. The young lady was as tall as Mrs. Bean, so I was nervous to go up and talk to her, but I managed to go up and actually start the conversation.

"Hi. My name is Lily. I may be coming to Juilliard next fall when I graduate high school. What is your name?"

"My name is Angie. It is nice to meet you, Lily. I heard you are an amazing dancer. I can't wait to see if what I heard is true, I have high expectations."

"You won't be disappointed, I can guarantee you, Angie."

"I don't think I will either. Well, I need to get going, but I will see you tomorrow at the big dance show."

As Angie walked away, I had a confused look on my face, because I didn't know what she meant by the big dance show. I thought she made a mistake, but then Mrs. Bean cleared up everything for me.

"I forgot to tell you, Lily, but tonight I set it up to where you are practicing with some of the best dancers, who went through my program in previous years, and you will be working on a dance routine to perform tomorrow afternoon before you leave. You will perform in front of the entire college."

My jaw dropped all the way to the ground. "Are you serious? I don't know if I can do that."

"I'm positive, Lily. If you are as good as everyone makes you out to be, you will do perfectly at this performance."

"If you say so, Mrs. Bean. When do I rehearse?"

"In two hours. You are going to go eat now, then go to practice, so you will want to eat light, and not have a heavy meal as you know."

"Yes, I know. Dancers should always eat light, especially before a practice or a performance."

"I will walk you to the dining hall."

As we were walking, I got a text from Amiah.

Hey, Lily. How have you been?

I've been good. How about you?

I've been good as well. Quick question. Where are you?

I'm at Juilliard in New York City. Why?

Look behind you.

When I looked behind me, I couldn't believe my eyes. It was Amiah! I squealed and ran up to her.

"What in the world are you doing here, Amiah?"

"I got accepted here for dance. What are you doing here, Lily?"

"I got accepted here as well for the dance program!"

Both Amiah and I got all excited and started jumping up and down. We couldn't believe we both got accepted to the same college for the same exact dance program.

"Are you going here for sure, Amiah?"

"I am! Are you, Lily?"

"Now I am since you are coming here. We have so much to catch up on. Want to eat dinner together?"

"Sure, Lily!"

The whole duration of dinner, Amiah and I caught up on things that had been going on in California and talked more about the Emmaline situation. In my mind, I still couldn't believe my best friend got accepted into the same school as I did. I mean, she was a better dancer than I was, but I didn't think she would want to be so far away from home for college. Amiah always liked to stay closer to home, because she was afraid if something were to happen with her family, she wouldn't be able to get back in time before something bad happened.

Amiah was in the middle of a story when I blacked out for a few minutes. When I woke up, Amiah was staring at me. I didn't know what happened, but all I did know was Amiah was waiting for me to answer something. I tried to quickly change the topic.

"Amiah, let's get going so we aren't late for rehearsal."

"Okay, Lily." Amiah looked confused but went along with what I wanted to do.

When we got to the rehearsal there were ten other dancers already warming up. Amiah and I decided to go and join in with them without any instructions on what we needed to do. We wanted to impress them.

The one young lady realized what we did, and got everyone else to look at what we were doing. They were impressed, to say the least. Everyone started warming up again for a few minutes after they admired us for a moment.

At about seven o'clock, we finally got started. A couple of the other girls that were starting the program next fall joined us as well.

"Welcome, everyone. My name is Annie. I first wanted to thank all of you for coming to this rehearsal, so we could practice for the Spring Performance we put on at Juilliard every year. We are going to practice for the next two hours, or until we can get this dance routine perfect. I have high expectations for all you girls. The song we are going to perform tomorrow is 'All About That Bass' by Meghan Trainor."

In my head, this was going to be easy, since Amiah and I danced to this song all the time when we are together. I couldn't wait to perform it the next day.

As the night came to a finish, I was getting pretty tired. I was staying on campus in one of the dorm rooms, with a girl who wanted to be my host for the night. By ten o'clock, I was ready for bed and almost asleep. I went right to sleep, I was excited about the performance and wanted it to come faster.

I slept pretty well until in the middle of the night I got woken up by a text from my dad saying;

Lily. I don't want you worrying while you are on your college visit with your dance team, but your sister is missing. Her boyfriend said she was supposed to return home yesterday around eight in the morning, but she never showed up. The only reason you are just now finding out about this is, that we were giving it a day to see if she was just taking a break from reality for a while like she usually does, but we have contacted her friends, and they haven't heard from her either. We are doing everything we can to find her, but we knew you should probably know. We will see you when you get back from your trip tomorrow evening.

After reading the text, I automatically texted Amiah to tell her. The way she responded was practically the same way I reacted. We both stayed up the rest of the night trying to keep each other calm. Before we both knew it, we had to be up for the day, since we performed at noon.

At breakfast, as soon as I saw Amiah, we both started crying our eyes out. We couldn't believe my sister was missing. When my host, Allysa, saw us crying, she came rushing over to us to see what was wrong.

"Lily, what is going on?"

I showed Allysa the text, and when she was done reading, she gave both Amiah and I a hug and tried to calm us down.

"I'm so sorry, girls. Getting this text, I know must be hard for you. You girls are in no shape to perform today. I'll go tell Mrs. Bean the situation, and she won't make you guys perform."

I stopped Allysa before she got too far. "No, Allysa, it's okay. We will be okay to perform. We can promise you."

"Are you sure, Lily?"

"We are sure. We have performed under similar conditions before."

"Okay, Lily. If you or Amiah need anything, let me know."

"Okay. Thank you, Allysa."

After the conversation, Amiah and I tried to eat some breakfast, so we wouldn't dance on empty stomachs. Breakfast went slowly. Amiah and I barely talked to each other. We kept on thinking about my sister and what could happen if we didn't find her. I couldn't bear the thought of losing my sister. Even though Maddy and I didn't get along sometimes, I still loved her.

Breakfast lasted until ten, then we had to go and get ready for the performance. From ten to the end of the performance, I knew I needed to focus on the performance only, so I could be the best I could be.

As noon came upon me, I had to be ready to perform. I was on stage in my spot, when all of a sudden, Allysa and a couple of the other girls grabbed Amiah and I and took us over to the corner, and prayed for us before we started. The girls praying for us was one of the most amazing things they could have done for us. Allysa knew exactly what I needed at that point in time, because I was losing faith. I didn't know how God could let something like this happen to my family, but after praying, I felt like I needed to trust God with the situation. He knows what He is doing and always will. After the prayer, we got right back in our spots and prepared for the amazing performance we practiced so hard for.

The performance lasted about a half-hour, and after we performed our song a couple of the other girls had a routine they did. Mrs. Bean introduced myself and Amiah in front of everyone, letting them know we would be the newest members of the team, starting in the fall. I couldn't believe Mrs. Bean would do that. I didn't have a problem with it, but I could tell Amiah did. With Amiah's anxiety, she hated to get praise in front of a huge crowd. I saw her hands starting to get sweaty, her legs were shaking, and her face was as bright as a tomato. When Mrs. Bean was done talking, Amiah ran off the stage, so did I. We had to try and hide from Mrs. Bean that Amiah had anxiety and hated to be in front of big crowds. If Mrs. Bean ever found out, she would probably take Amiah's scholarship away, and that would tear Amiah to pieces. In order to make sure no one ever found out, Amiah had to try and control herself. We went to the edge of the stage, hugged, and went back to our spots quickly.

When two o'clock came around, Amiah and I had to say our goodbyes. Her mom was picking her up, while I had to head back to the airport to catch my flight, which took off at nine that night. Saying goodbye was one of the hardest things I had to do because all I wanted was Amiah to come back to France with me, and help find Maddy. I knew it was best if I went alone, though. Amiah and I would see each other again in the Fall. I still couldn't believe what I was going home to. I was hoping the flight would be quicker than the flight to New York was.

I got through the airport with about an hour until my flight took off. I put my headphones in and listened to music for the entire time. I didn't want to talk to anyone, so I put my phone on airplane mode. I just wanted to stay in New York and hide away until I knew for sure I would go home and my sister would be there. I knew that wasn't how I needed to deal with this, though. My parents needed me during this time. I just couldn't wait until I could hear my sister's voice again. The next twenty-four hours were a blur.

Chapter 9

When I got back to the airport in France, I was supposed to call my parents to let them know I made it and needed to be picked up. I knew they were going through a rough time already, so I figured since I still had money left from my trip I could use the rest to find another way home, and not add on to the pressure my parents were going through. I didn't want to use any more of my money though, and I knew there was one person who would do anything for me, no matter what the situation was. This person was Mrs. Nitch. When I went to call her, my phone died, so I had no way of getting a hold of her. I tried to remember her phone number, but for some reason, my mind was going blank. I searched through my bag to see if I put something in there with her number on it. I looked for a good twenty minutes until I realized I had her phone number on a slip of paper, which was in my phone case. I took apart my phone case, and the paper was still there intact. I couldn't believe it. I went up to one of the workers at the airport and asked if they could show me where the payphone was.

The phone rang for about thirty seconds until some strange man answered the phone. I nervously asked if Mrs. Nitch was there.

The man answered rudely, "Who is this and why do you want Mrs. Nitch? She isn't allowed to talk to anyone, so if you could please, not call back."

I wanted to cry because something was wrong with Mrs. Nitch. There were several things that caught me off guard and made me afraid there was something not right going on. First, Mrs. Nitch usually always answered her phone, because she hated other people using her phone. Second, I don't remember

Mrs. Nitch ever mentioning something about a guy being in her life. She was recently divorced because her ex was having an affair with another woman for eight years. Finally, Mrs. Nitch always had time for me and any of the other girls. She would always drop what she was doing to come to help us if we were in some sort of trouble. With all of these things, I came to the conclusion that Mrs. Nitch was possibly being held hostage, and I needed to try and go save her, but at the same time, I wanted to get home, because I knew my parents needed me with everything going on with Maddy. I knew what I wanted to do.

I would first find a way to Mrs. Nitch's house and see what was going on there, then after all of that is figured out, then maybe she will be able to help me with my situation. I called the taxi and went to Mrs. Nitch's. The only way I knew where she lived was because, about a month ago, she invited all the girls on the dance team to spend the night at her house, so we could have team bonding. That night was one of the funniest days I have had ever since I started dancing. It took the taxi twenty minutes to get to the airport. When it got there, I got in and told the driver where I needed to go. I listened to music the whole way there, so I could get my mind prepared for what I was about to encounter.

When I got to the house, I quietly walked up to the sidewalk, which was leading to her house. There was only one light on, and the light was coming from her bedroom. I walked around the house and looked through all of the windows to make sure that once I entered the house, I wasn't going to run into an unexpected guest. As far as I could see there was nothing in front of the house. Once I got to the back of the house, it was an entirely different story. On the back porch, I saw a trail of blood. I didn't wait to see anything else, I ran into the house and up to the bedroom. I couldn't believe it. Laying against the wall was Mrs. Nitch, still breathing, but barely. She had cuts on her legs and was tied up to the post at the head of her bed. I went over to make sure she could still talk, but I didn't waste any time and called 1-1-2. I knew I wasn't allowed to touch anything, because, if I did, my DNA would be all over the crime scene, and I didn't want to be considered a suspect for a crime I didn't commit.

The police and ambulance got to the house in about five minutes. They asked me what happened and I told them the whole story. They got Mrs. Nitch into the ambulance, while the police stayed back to ask me questions and collect evidence from the house. I had to go down to the police station to get my fingerprints and write a statement of what I saw and did. After everything, they took me back home and said they would call me if they needed anything else from me. When I got home, I entered into another dramatic event.

My parents were on the couch holding each other and crying. I knew this event could only mean a couple of options. Either they found my sister and I no longer have a sister, or they have no leads on where she could be. I wanted to know, but at the same time, I didn't. They didn't realize I came in, so I went over to join the hug. When they felt me around them, they handed me a letter. The letter contained a picture of my sister locked up and these words.

I have your little girl, Maddy. She is quite beautiful if I say so myself. She has a true talent for dancing and has been showing me everything she knows. I couldn't wait to get my hands on her. Lately, though, she hasn't been wanting to listen or do what I want her to do. I decided to teach her a lesson. If she starts listening again, she will keep her wishes and stay alive. If she doesn't start listening, both her and your grandbaby will be dead within a week, I also need

85

twenty thousand dollars by the end of the week, and since she can't give me the money, the money will have to come from you guys. According to her, you guys will do anything to see her alive and happy. If this is true, then you will do whatever it takes to make the money appear. You have exactly one week, to drop it off at this address. CS 70025, 85590 les Epesses. When you get there, at exactly midnight, you will take the money to where the circus performs, and in the middle of the ring, there will be a small black box. You will lift the box up, set the money down, and walk away slowly to the entrance of the ring, Once you get to the entrance, you will stand there and wait exactly ten minutes. I will come and collect the money. IF you follow my instruction exactly how I give them to you, I will lead you to where Maddy is. IF you don't do exactly what I say, you will never see your daughter again. You are also not allowed to get the police involved in any way. If you do, Maddy is gone. You are also to bring your daughter, Lily with you. Those are my only requests. I will see you in a week. Signed, Anonymous.

After reading the note, and seeing the picture, we knew we had to do something to save Maddy. The only problem is, we didn't have twenty thousand dollars just laying around anywhere. We barely had enough to make house payments each month. We knew we couldn't go to the police, but we had to get help from someone because we needed to get the money one way or another. I knew I had money saved up in my checking account, but I didn't have the twenty thousand we needed. I had an idea, but I didn't know how my parents would react to my suggestion.

"Mom, I have an idea. It is a long shot but it is a shot worth taking. Why don't we call grandma and grandpa to see if they can help us any? You know they will do anything for Maddy."

"That is a good idea, Lily, but I don't think they have the amount of money we need."

86

"You never know, though."

My parents got suspicious. "Lily, do you know something we don't?"

When they asked that question, I had to come up with an answer, because I did know something, but I promised grandma and grandpa I wouldn't tell my parents about the secret stash of money they have been putting away for the last ten years now.

"No, I don't. I promise." I couldn't believe I lied right through my white teeth again.

"Okay, Lily. We will call them now."

"Okay. Can I go for a walk?"

"Go ahead, Lily, but be back before dinner."

"Okay."

I knew exactly where I wanted to go. I wanted to go back to the crime scene of Mrs. Nitch, but I knew it was probably best I didn't. Instead, I started walking to the park to get my mind off of things. Plus the park was one of Maddy's favorite places to go and dance for all the little kids. I wanted to carry on her tradition, until we found her, and brought her home all in one piece.

When I got to the park, there were about two dozen kids here, running around and playing ball. I got my phone out and turned on the song 'Wherever I Go' by Miley Cyrus. This was the song I was going to use to make a slideshow, so I can show my parents at the right time, to let them know I'm leaving for Juilliard next fall.

As soon as the music started, all the kids stopped what they were doing and came running over to me to see what I was doing. I started my routine and all the kids calmly organized themselves into the grass to sit and watch me dance. This alone gave me the inspiration to continue what I was doing. This far into my dancing career, the only reason I wanted to continue was to entertain people and make them happy with my dancing.

I just got finished with my routine when I got a phone call from the police. They asked me if I could come down to the station, so I could talk to them. I agreed since I still had about an hour until I had to be back home. I knew there was a shortcut from the park to the police station, which made the trip less than ten minutes, instead of a half-hour walk. Taking time into consideration, I knew my best bet would be to take the shortcut, so I could make it to the police station, and back home before time was up. I put my headphones back on and was on my way.

The whole way to the police station, I came up with a couple of theories of why the police needed me there. They either found the person who did it, they need to ask me a couple of more questions, or they thought I did it. I was hoping one of my first two theories were right, and they didn't consider me a suspect at all. Even thinking about the third option got my heart beating. I tried to breathe in and out, so I wouldn't get overwhelmed thinking about it. I knew it was close to impossible they thought of me as a suspect. The only evidence they could put towards it is my fingerprints on the back door, my shoe prints leading up to the bedroom, and if any dirt from my fingernails got on Mrs. Nitch's skin when I was checking to see if she was still breathing. Those are the only things they could have against me though. By the time I got to the police station, there was a Sous-Brigadier, or Sergeant, by the entrance waiting for me. I recognized the face, because it was Sergeant Abreo. She was at the crime scene and asked me a couple of questions. By the looks on her face, she didn't have good news for me. Once I approached her, she tried to talk, but once she opened her mouth she couldn't speak any words at first.

"Hi, Lily."

"What's going on? Is Mrs. Nitch okay?"

"I'm afraid I have some bad news for you."

I started to have tears going down my face because I knew exactly what she was going to say at that point. "She's not going to make it. Is she?"

Sergeant Abreo pulled me into her arms and whispered into my ear, "I'm afraid not, Lily."

Once I pulled myself away, I decided to run to the hospital where Mrs. Nitch was. There was only one local hospital where I lived. Sergeant Abreo got in her cruiser and came rushing after me. Once she caught up to me, she told me to get in so she could take me to the hospital, so I didn't make any dumb decisions since I was upset.

The whole ride to the hospital was nothing but silence. I usually hated the silence, but this time I didn't mind it. I listened to the cool air blowing and listened to all the little noises which surrounded me. When we got to the hospital, I didn't even take a second to unbuckle and rushed into the hospital, to try and find Mrs. Nitch, I ran up to the receptionist to figure out where I needed to go.

"I'm looking for Mrs. Nitch."

"Hi. She is in room four forty-five on the fourth floor."

"Thank you."

I didn't wait for Sergeant Abreo to catch up before I went to the room. When I got to the room, I barged in without knocking, so I could see her. The moment I saw Mrs. Nitch, I knew she was fighting to stay alive. I couldn't stand to see her like this. It was killing me, though I knew whatever happened next was for the best. I knew God had control of this situation. He did for Mrs. Marine.

I gave Mrs. Nitch a huge hug, and at the moment, I could feel Mrs. Nitch taking her last breath here on Earth. I knew from then on out dancing would mean a whole other thing to me.

Chapter 10

When I got home, my parents looked at me with a worried look on their faces. "Lily. We called Grandma and Grandpa, and they didn't have the money. They said they would help us a little bit by transferring half of the cash into our accounts tonight, but we have to try and figure out where to get the other half of the money that we need. Do you have any ideas, Lily?"

"Not at the moment, Mom. If I come up with anything, I'll let you know."

"Thank you, Lily. Don't worry too much about it, though. We will find Maddy one way or another with or without the money. We can promise you that. Both you and your sister mean the world to us, and we won't let anything bad happen to either of you. I have my wedding ring I can sell and get the rest of the money. Don't worry about anything. We got it taken care of."

"Thank you, Mom."

I went back up to my room to think about everything that had happened in the last forty-eight hours. I kept thinking about Maddy, though. I wanted my sister back, and even though I wished Mrs. Nitch was here, Maddy was family, and there was still hope in finding her to bring her back home where she belonged.

I went into Maddy's room and dug out the scrapbook that she was in the progress of making. It was supposed to capture all of the moments of our family and everyone's successes. It had a baby bracelet from when she first came home from the hospital, it had a picture of her on her first birthday, and a picture of me at my first dance recital. I didn't realize that she took that and put it in there. Maddy was particular about who made it into her scrapbook. Usually, it was all about her, and no one else. Still, when it came down to it, if there was an option between her living and family, she would choose her family living. That is another reason why I knew we needed to find Maddy without putting any of the other family into danger.

The next couple of nights were rough in terms of trying to get any sleep. My mind was all over the place and wondering about what was going to happen next. Not only about me but my whole family. Were we going to ever find Maddy? Was the person that wrote that letter telling us the truth that if we did what they wanted us to, then they would give us back Maddy? Was she even still alive? Were they really going to go after our family if they didn't get what they asked for? These questions were floating around in my mind like there was no gravity holding them down, and they were doing whatever they wanted to do. Maddy wasn't the only person I had on my mind either. Mrs. Nitch was also on my mind. Who could have done such a terrible thing to her? She was such a nice person who wouldn't harm a fly or any creature in that matter.

I eventually did figure out that her funeral and calling hours were on that Friday that my parents and I were supposed to go see about finding Maddy. There was no way I was going to miss finding my sister. Still, I also wanted to attend the funeral for one of the best high school dance teachers in the country, in my opinion. I had to come up with a way that I could attend both things and not come into any conflicts. It took a couple of crumbled pieces of paper, three cups of coffee, and a music session to come up with the perfect plan.

My parents said we weren't going to leave until about one that afternoon, and the funeral was at noon. So I would get to the funeral a couple minutes earlier just so that I could give my condolences to the family. Then I could come back home to get ready to go see Maddy again. I was hoping this would work because I still thought that it wasn't a good idea for me to be left alone. Who knows if this person who has Maddy was dangerous and would really come after my family or me if they didn't get what they wanted to the first time that they asked. It was a risk worth taking because there was no way that I was going to miss this funeral just because I was paranoid. I doubt the person was earnest about anything they said in the letter. They would have to have my sister with them, so he didn't want to take the chance of her escaping when they were gone, and she was left alone. I didn't think they were that dumb; if they were, then they would have already given up their identity, and we would have my sister back home where she belonged.

In the next few days, the whole family stayed in the house most of the time unless we absolutely needed to go out. We were all paranoid since we couldn't reach out for help because this mysterious person had us terrified.

The morning finally came that we had to face our fears and go save Maddy. We all got up around eight that morning. I got ready for the funeral. It was hard because I didn't have anything black to wear and I knew that it was a tradition to wear black to occasions like this. I knew Maddy had plenty of black dresses, but I didn't feel comfortable going into her closet to try and find something to wear. I would feel miserable doing that knowing that there may be a chance that I won't ever see my sister again. I had to try and get that thought out of my mind. I had to keep positive thoughts and think to myself that I was going to find her. The more I thought about it, I knew I needed to find something to wear, and so I did decide to go through Maddy's closet and find an outfit. It only took a matter of two minutes to find something to wear. There was a black dress that Maddy wore to one of her first high school dance recitals. It was a unique dress for the whole family because it has been in my family for generations. It went back to my great-great-great-grandma and has been handed down after each person turned eighteen. To them, it was a sign of adulthood.

Once I put the dress on, I walked into the restroom just to see how I looked. When I saw myself in the mirror, I shed a tear or two. I looked just like Maddy. I had long red hair that was always straight and shiny. I had a couple freckles on my right cheek. I had a dimple as well. We both got that from our father. I also had bright blue eyes. I don't know where I got those from because I was the only one in our family that had blue eyes. Maddy had green eyes, and both of my parents had brown eyes. It was kind of cool to have blue eyes because that is what made me different from Maddy. However, even with that difference, we still looked like identical twins except for the age difference. I couldn't help but break down crying. My parents came rushing in to see what was going on. They saw that I had on Maddy's dress and came running over to hug me. They started crying as well. I knew today was going to be a long and rough day for everyone. We sat on the edge of Maddy's bed for a couple minutes, just comforting each other. We were reassuring each other that everything was going to be okay, no matter what came in our way and happened.

At about eleven-thirty, my parents took me to the funeral. When I got there, everyone was surrounding the casket. I ran over to see what everyone was looking at. Right when I got there, there was a note attached to the coffin. The letter was made out to me. It said:

I am not done. I still am on the loose and won't stop until I get what I want. Watch out, Lily.

When I saw that my legs started shaking, my face got red, and my voice was shaky to the point where I could barely speak. I said my condolences to the family but then quickly took the note and ran out of the building. I was looking all around for someone that was obviously following me or knew that I was going to be here today. I didn't want to think that I had an enemy, but by the looks of it, I had an enemy and a stalker. My parents saw that I was upset and came to me asking what was going on. After I told them, we immediately went to the police station to tell them what was going on. I was in danger, and we couldn't risk anything happening to me.

When we got to the police station, we told them of all the events that have happened leading up to this day. We then handed them both letters that had come into our possession. They were written by the same person, but we didn't know who it was because they signed it anonymously. The Sous-Brigadier in charge took the notes and sent them to the lab to check for fingerprints and see if they could analyze the handwriting. While we were there, they had to take our prints just so if they found fingerprints on the paper, they could check to see if the fingerprints were ours or the person who wrote the note. It took about a half-hour for everything to get done. Right when we were about to leave to go and find Maddy, one of the officers in command stopped us.

"Hey. My name is Gardien de la Paix Allemand. I don't think that you guys should follow through with this plan to go to this random place without some law enforcement involved.

We know that you were told not to bring any, but if you don't, we don't think you will come back with either daughter if we are completely honest with each other. Let me follow you guys, that way I can keep your family safe and bring your other daughter Maddy back to where she belongs."

Without hesitation, we agreed to have Officer Allemand come along. It was a long ride to the amusement park. We cried some, but we didn't dare speak to each other because we knew that once we got upset, the words that came out of our mouths had a chance of hurting someone when we didn't mean it.

We got to the place we had to meet this person at eleven fifty-nine, a minute before we had to complete their request. My parents got the money somehow, but they wouldn't tell me who or how they got it. They did bring me with them, but Officer Allemand was right behind us. That way, if this person did try and pull something on me, I would be safe because they would be right there to help me.

Once the clock struck midnight, my parents walked to the middle of the circus ring. They lifted up the box that was there, set down the money, carefully put the lid back down, and strolled back to the entrance. We waited there for about ten minutes to see if this person was going to show up. Around twelve ten, we finally saw an all-black figure slowly make its way to the middle of the ring. It was utterly silent as they lifted up the box to make sure that everything was there. Once they collected the money that was there, they quickly but quietly made it back to where they came from. Something was strange, though, because Maddy was nowhere in sight. We didn't think that they could have figured out that the police were involved though, so we knew there was something up. The mystery person promised that if we did what they wanted and gave them the money, then we would have Maddy back with us. When I didn't see Maddy, I ran over to where the person entered, and I couldn't believe what I was looking at.

Chapter 11

Right there in front of me was Maddy but not the Maddy that I knew. It wasn't my sister or at least didn't look like my sister. She had cuts all over her body, she was bleeding from her head, she had a black eye, and was all tied up to a pole that was holding the building up. I yelled for my parents and Officer Allemand over for assistance. When they got over to where I was, my parents automatically fell to their knees and started crying. Officer Allemand called for backup so we could get Maddy to the nearest hospital and quick to get her checked out thoroughly. I tried to help Maddy stay awake until the ambulance arrived there. I knew how to help clean her up a little bit since I was in a similar situation as her recently. It only took the emergency vehicles about four and a half minutes to get to where we were. Once they got there, I got out of the way so that they could do their jobs.

While they were getting her into an ambulance, I went into a faraway corner and started to pray to God. I knew my sister had a will that she wasn't going to let anything or anyone get in her way of achieving her goal. She and I had that in common. Once I got alone in a corner, I let all of my emotions out to God.

"Dear Heavenly Father. I come to You and ask you to heal my sister. I don't know what happened to her and no one but You may ever know what happened, but I know that You can use her for Your Glory in one way or another. I pray that You can use me to help her, as well. In all this, I pray in Jesus' name, Amen."

As I got done with praying, I felt a hand on my shoulder. Sometime during my praying, my father came over and joined me. He was almost in tears, but this time they were happy tears instead of tears of sadness.

"Hey, Princess. That was so sweet of you to pray for your sister. It was nice hearing you pray. You haven't prayed or been to church in a while, and so I didn't know if I would ever hear you pray again."

"Thanks, Dad. Yeah, I have been losing faith lately, especially during everything with Maddy. I didn't think that we were going to find her or if we did, we weren't going to receive good news. After seeing her, I knew that was a sign of something. Yes, when we found her, she wasn't in the best conditions, but we still found her, and that is all that matters to me. I can't wait to have my big sister back home with us where she belongs."

"Same here, Princess. Let's go and head to the hospital so we can be with your sister. Your mom went in the ambulance with her so that she will join us there."

"Okay, Dad. Let's go."

During the car ride to the hospital, Officer Allemand followed us, so he made sure we made it there safely. My Dad and I also tried to remember some of the stories we had with Maddy; that way we kept a positive vibe. We didn't need any negative thoughts anymore since we had our family back together. The ride to the hospital took about fifteen minutes. We didn't go to the one by our house since we needed to get Maddy checked out as soon as we could, and our house was seven hours away from where we were.

Once we got to the hospital, Maddy was already up in a room. She was sleeping, but they had her hooked up to a heart monitor and other machines. If there was any drastic change in her vital signs, they could wake her up before anything happened. It was hard to sleep, but my parents and I took shifts of who was to stay awake and who could get some sleep. We each slept for two hours and then switched off. My parents had the first shift to staying awake with Maddy. They thought I would need more sleep because not only did I go through today worrying about Maddy, but I also had to go to a funeral. I fell asleep right away.

Once I was in a deep sleep, I started dreaming of me moving to New York to attend Juilliard. The day I arrived, it was raining, but it was cool. I got to the apartment that the school provided. I greeted Amiah, who arrived a day earlier. She was already settled into the studio. We spent the day catching up with each other and exploring New York because the next day we were to start classes at Juilliard. We spent the whole day shopping and getting things for the apartment like food and some other knick-knacks. It was almost the perfect day until something terrible happened. One minute I was with Amiah, and the other I wasn't. I woke up at that time because I got scared. I still had a half-hour that I could sleep, but I decided to give that up and have my parents go to sleep.

When my parents fell asleep is when Maddy woke up. When she opened her eyes, I was right there by her side. She looked over at me with her big green beautiful eyes. I missed those eyes so much. She signaled for me to come even closer so that she could tell me something in private. I got as close to her as I possibly could. When I got by her ear, she whispered, "I'm a potato."

After she said that, we both started laughing hysterically loud because she was still on some kind of medicine that made her tired and, in some form, high. When we were both done laughing I kissed her on the forehead and she slowly went right back to sleep. I was so glad to be able to see my sister again.

The next morning when my parents got up, they went out to the closest restaurant to get some breakfast for everyone. I had pancakes, sausage, bacon, and some orange juice. Maddy had to be careful about what she ate and drank because the doctors evaluated her and came to the conclusion that she had alcohol poisoning, and she kept vomiting after waking up. It was hard for Maddy because she was a real food addict and would eat anything and everything that she could get her hands on, but she always managed to stay skinny no matter what. The doctors also had to be careful because they did figure out as well that Maddy was pregnant. When Maddy could remember events that happened, she said that she puked most of the alcohol up when her kidnapper forced her to drink, but some of it still got in her system. She could barely remember a lot of the events, especially when detectives came to talk to her to try and figure out who this mystery person was.

Maddy honestly didn't know who the person was but knew it was a male just by the sound of their voice and the things that he did to her when he wasn't forcing her to dance for him. He always wore a mask when he was around her. There was one thing that Maddy told us that caught everyone's attention. She said that the guy told us to watch our backs because he only wants me now. After hearing that I started having a panic attack. I couldn't believe that the person who did this to my sister wanted to come after me and either do the same things that he did to her to me or worse. My parents and I didn't know what to think.

The detective did take my parents into the hallway to talk about some options that she thought would be best for my family and me. They were in that hallway for a good twenty five minutes. It was hard to focus on their lips of what they were saying since I was still worried about what was going to happen next. When everyone came inside the room, the detective came over to try and talk to Maddy more while my parents pulled me out into the hallway.

"Maddy. After talking with Detective Yount, we came up with a solution. We are going to send you back to California in the summer to live with your grandparents. We aren't wanting to risk anything happening to you. So we are going to try and call later today and arrange everything. How does this sound?"

"I like the sound of that plan, but I got a better one. Want to hear it?"

"Sure, Lily, but this isn't really in for discussion. We are looking out for what is best for you and your safety."

"I know, Mom, but you are going to like this plan, I think."

"Okay. Let's hear it."

"Okay. Well, I was trying to find the right time to tell you guys this, but the time just never seemed to be right with everything that went down. At first, you guys are probably going to yell at me, but in the end, it is going to be worth it."

"Liliana, get on with your idea."

"Okay. When I told you guys that I was going with my dance team to Chicago, I lied. I went to New York to Juilliard, but I went by myself. The reason for that is because I got accepted into one of their prestigious dance schools as a Freshman. I wanted to visit the school for myself. Well, you will never believe who also got accepted into the same program. Amiah! She surprised me, and she is going there in the fall. I propose that I stay with you guys until the beginning semester at Juilliard. Then I can go to Juilliard and stay with Amiah at the apartment that the school had for us. I know that I'll only be seventeen still at the time but this is an opportunity of a lifetime. I don't want to miss this, so can I please do this?"

"First, Lily, you are grounded for the next week for lying to us. Second, you will have to let me and your father talk about this matter. It isn't something that is going to be easy, but we will consider everything. We will have a decision for you by the end of this week."

"Okay. I accept my punishment because I know what I did was wrong, and I deserve everything that I deserve. Thank you for even considering this. I won't bother you again about the plan until you tell me your answer."

The next week went fast. That Friday, my mom called me down while I was doing homework.

"Lily. Your dad and I have been thinking. We know how much dancing means to you, and going to Juilliard is a dream of a lifetime. We don't want to stop you from achieving your dreams. We know since Maddy made the mistake of not going to Juilliard, we don't want you not to go just because we were stubborn and wanting you to be safe. The answer to whether or not you can go to Juilliard in the fall is yes. We've also arranged for you to stay with Amiah during the summer."

When my parents said that, I hugged them and ran upstairs to call Amiah to tell her the good news.

Once I got on the phone, Amiah and I talked for three hours, talking about how it was going to be awesome going to the same college. We still couldn't believe that this was happening. Dancing was our dream, and we couldn't wait to see where it took us in the future.

Around nine-thirty that night my mom had to come and cut the conversation off because I had to get some sleep since I had school the next week. That was a word that was never going to be the same again. Dance was never going to be the same either. Mrs. Nitch was one of the only people that kept me going to school because she had a way of making it fun, and even when I wasn't in her dance class, she still held my focus. It was going to be hard to do that. The only good thing is that I only had one more week of school and then it was summer. We had exams all week, though. I knew I wasn't going to do well but decided to at least try and make it through, so I graduated high school. I needed to graduate because if I didn't graduate, I couldn't go to Juilliard next year. Amiah was coming to France to watch me graduate. Then I was going back with her to watch her graduation. She was my motivation to get through the week.

When my alarm clock went off on Monday, I hit the snooze five times before I got up. It was a sunny day, and so the sun was shining brightly into my room. I grabbed my favorite Eiffel Tower t-shirt and a skirt that I bought at a souvenir shop the other day. I walked downstairs to be greeted by my parents and Maddy, who was setting the table for breakfast. There were waffles, pancakes, sausage, bacon, toast, and orange juice all on the table ready to be eaten. I didn't take a second look and ran down the stairs. I was starving. My parents looked at me like I was crazy. When in reality, I wanted a good breakfast so I could think about my exams and pass all of them with flying colors. We all sat down to eat for about twenty minutes before I had to get ready and leave for school. My dad took me to school so I wouldn't have to walk. It only took five minutes for us to get to school. Before I got out of the car, I kissed him on the cheek and left. I saw a couple of my friends in my math class that I wanted to catch up with to talk about our summer plans. I knew this week was going to be a good one. The week went by fast.

Chapter 12

That Friday, once I got up, I got ready right away. I wanted to get to school faster and get home sooner. That way, when I got back, Amiah would already be here waiting for me. My mom was supposed to pick her up on her lunch break from the airport. I couldn't wait to see my best friend again, but before I went downstairs, I heard a voice that wasn't my parents or Maddy's. The sound was familiar, though. I didn't think my ears would deceive me and so I ran downstairs, and when I got there, I couldn't believe what I was seeing. Amiah was already here. Eight hours early! She didn't realize that I was up already, so I ran over to her and jumped on her back. She about fell face-first into my mom, who was standing in front of her talking. Amiah kept her balance, though, and grabbed onto my legs to hold me up on her back. We both started bursting out laughing. Maddy looked at us both like we had finally lost our minds and went insane. After we could eventually catch our breath, I started an actual conversation.

"What are you already doing here, Amiah? I thought you weren't supposed to get here until after school today."

"I wasn't supposed to, but I guess my mom got my flight mixed up. My plane took off Thursday afternoon instead of Thursday evening. That is what brought me here as early as it did. Aren't you glad to see me, though?"

"I am, I just wasn't expecting to see you until after I got home from school. What are you going to do all day while I'm not here?"

"Well, Maddy said that she would take me shopping since she still isn't allowed to go to college for another couple weeks, as you already knew this."

"Okay. Well, that is good to hear. I hope you two have fun."

I then turned to Maddy, and with as dangerous of a face that I could make, I told her, "I want Amiah back the minute I step in the door this afternoon." I couldn't keep the serious face for very long. After about thirty seconds, everyone started cracking up laughing again. I then hugged Amiah back and got ready to catch the bus to school. My Dad already left for work, and my mom couldn't take me, and so I could only catch the bus to get to school, as they didn't think it was safe for me to walk alone now. Right when I stepped into the school doors, it was chaotic everywhere I looked.

Everyone was going around getting pictures with friends and teachers, cleaning out their lockers, and taking all of the posters that were hung up on the walls down. I didn't have that many friends at that school, so I didn't have much to get done. The only things that were on my mind the whole day were Amiah and graduation. I wanted to see my best friend. I also couldn't wait to walk across the stage the next day to receive a braver des collèges. All of my family were flying to France just to watch me graduate. It was a big day for not only me but for my family as well. I would be the only one that will have walked across a stage to graduate. Neither of my parents graduated high school. Maddy graduated but never walked across the stage because the day she was supposed to, she got sick and wasn't allowed walking. That day was a massive disappointment for everyone. I wasn't anywhere near ill, so I was on the right track to a considerable achievement.

The school day went by slowly, though, just because there were a lot of emotions, and we barely did any work in our classes since it was the last day. Plus, I think the teachers were just as ready as we were to get the heck out of that place. A lot of us dancers though, during the last hour and a half of school, went to the dance room. We wanted to feel what it was like to be in there again. We had been trying to avoid the place as much as we possibly could. It was easy half the time since we didn't have Mrs. Nitch around. The school didn't bother getting a new dance instructor at the end of the year, so ever since the incident happened, we quit dancing for a while. When we were supposed to have dance classes, we would just meet on the lawn of the school and talk or study together. We all knew though that we needed to step into the dance room one last time as a team. When we walked in there, we all shed a tear or two. We couldn't believe that we were Seniors and that the one teacher that inspired us all to dance better wasn't even around to give us a send-off.

Adria had a great idea, though. She suggested that we all do the routine to the song 'The Climb' one last time since it was Mrs. Nitch's favorite routine that we did. I took over and helped get the team organized and into their spots. When we all were ready, I got out the music player and put the CD in. We all started to dance our hearts out. As the last minute of the song was playing, some people were gathering at the door to watch us. I didn't even notice them until I did a one-eighty spin. I got the biggest smile on my face when I saw all of the people. I couldn't believe that everyone wanted to watch us. All the girls finished off the routine strong.

When we all finished, we came together as a team and did a big group hug. We cried a little, but it was all worth it. The sun was beaming in the room. We took that as a signal that Mrs. Nitch was watching over us. All of a sudden, the last bell rang, and it was time to go home. All the other students in the school ran out of the school like a wild pack of hyenas. The team waited five minutes, and then we walked out together.

We said our last goodbyes and exchanged contacts; that way we wouldn't stop talking just because we all moved on with our lives.

I started walking home, thinking about everything that went on today. I had to admit that yes, I had a rough start to the beginning of the year when I arrived. Still, all of the events that have happened made me stronger and formed me into the young lady that I am now.

After about ten minutes of walking, I saw Amiah walking towards me, crying her eyes out. I ran up to her with a worried look on my face.

"What's wrong, Amiah?"

At first, she didn't say anything, but she gave me an angry look.

"Amiah, what is going on?"

"Why didn't you tell me! Were you expecting me not to find out?"

"What in the world are you talking about, Amiah?"

She put the last note that was from the anonymous person in my face. It was telling me how I should look out because he isn't going to stop until he gets what he wants.

"I'm sorry, Amiah. First, I didn't want to scare you, and secondly, we went to the police and got it all taken care of, so I didn't think there was anything to discuss."

"I'm sorry, Lily, that I'm overreacting. I care about you. I don't want to see anything happen to you. Especially if we are going to be going to New York City to attend Juilliard together."

"Amiah. Listen to me. The reason that I am allowed to go to Juilliard is that it will be safer there for me then it is here in France. Nothing is going to happen to you or me. We can protect each other. I know for a fact that I won't let anything happen to you. I can promise you that."

"I guess you are right, Lily. I'm sorry. I was overreacting. Do you accept my apology?"

"Yes, I do, Amiah. Now, let's get down to the important question. Do you want to go visit the Eiffel Tower since this is your first time in France?"

"Sure!"

"Okay. Follow me. It's only a couple blocks away."

I started running, and Amiah followed after me. We only had a couple of hours because that afternoon, around five, I had a graduation rehearsal that I had to attend. I didn't think about that, though. I wanted to focus my time on Amiah.

When we got the Eiffel tower, we stood in front of it for a couple of minutes to admire its look and beautiful appearance. We also took pictures while we were there. We wanted to capture this moment. We decided to race to see who could get to the top of the Eiffel Tower first. Since both Amiah and I ran cross country as well, we knew we would be a good competition for each other.

We stretched before we started so we wouldn't get hurt in the process. When we were ready, we were off. We had a lot of obstacles because there were a lot of tourists that were walking up the Eiffel Tower at the same time that we were racing. It was fun, though, because we got some people that started cheering us on and betting on which one of us was going to win. It took a total of ten minutes for us to get to the top of the second floor. We then had to see who could catch the elevator first so we could get to the top of the Eiffel Tower. We both got in a different elevator at the same time. Still, unfortunately, she beat me because my elevator was slower. It was all good, though, because we had people cheering. We were both out of breath. It was a lot of fun, but when I looked at my clock, I about died. It was already four-thirty, and I had to be at the school in a half-hour. That meant I had to get down the Tower and to the school as fast as I could.

I violently grabbed Amiah and told her I would explain on the way. We sprinted down the tower and out to the street. I had to try and quickly figure out how to get to the school because I hadn't figured out how to get to the school from the Eiffel Tower before. All I remember is we had to go past the seafood restaurant down the street, and then from there, it was only back roads. We got about ten minutes down the road when a familiar car pulled up to the side of the way. The windows rolled down, and it was my mom and sister. I was so glad to see them.

"Lily. You are going to be late for a graduation rehearsal. Get in. I will take you to school."

"Thank you, Mom. Amiah and I were having a lot of fun at the Eiffel Tower that we lost track of time."

"I'm glad you two are having fun, but you know how important tonight and tomorrow is, Lily. You cannot miss a rehearsal, or you don't walk with the rest of the Seniors tomorrow evening."

"Mom is right, Lily. I know I didn't get to walk with the rest of my friends, and I couldn't help that, but I don't want the same thing to happen to you."

"Thanks, Maddy. I won't miss graduation. Trust me. I have been waiting for this for months now. Graduation means that I'm one step closer to Juilliard."

"That's good, Lily. I'm so proud of you. I know that I gave up Juilliard because I was stupid in love with a guy that I'm not even sure loves me anymore. You are not stupid though, Lily. You are taking dance and your academics very seriously. I wish I had a mindset like you. Now let's get you through this next milestone of many."

"That means a lot to me, Maddy. You are not stupid either, Maddy. We all make mistakes that we regret, but we learn from them in one way or another."

"Thanks, Lily."

That conversation took just enough time for us to get to school. When we arrived, it was four fifty-five, and so I had five minutes to get into my cap and gown and find my place in line so we could go through the whole graduation ceremony. Some parents did stay to watch the practice so that they could get some pre-graduation photos. I didn't focus much on them, but there was one person that did catch my attention though. There was a young white Caucasian male that was sitting alone in the corner of the auditorium. Whenever I wasn't paying attention, he would only be looking at me. When I would look towards him, he would look away and act like nothing was happening. I tried to get it out of my mind because it was probably nothing. At the end of the rehearsal, everyone took off their cap and gown and made sure to put them away in the drama room's closet. I tried to stay close to other kids because I still wasn't sure about the man that was lurking around. I was just hoping he was one of the kids' parents.

That night when I got home, I was anxious, and Amiah knew that something was up because I was distant with everyone. Once we got up into my room to get ready for bed, she shut my door so no one would hear us talking.

"Lily, what in the world is wrong with you tonight? You have been acting strange ever since the graduation rehearsal. Did something happen during the rehearsal?"

"Not really," I went and opened my door just a little to make sure that no one was around and listening, and then I quietly shut the door again. "Okay, look, Amiah. I am going to tell you something, but you can not tell anyone. My parents don't even know. They already have a lot on their plate with my sister and everything. At the play rehearsal, there was this strange guy. He was sitting all alone, and when I wasn't paying attention, he would stare at me and then act like he wasn't doing anything wrong. Now, I may be overreacting, and he may have just had a kid in my class and was looking at them, but they were close to where I was. I'm trying to think that it was nothing, and so I am just trying to be extra careful of my surroundings. Please don't worry, Amiah. I will be okay even when we will be out of this country in two days. Do you trust me?"

"I trust you, Lily. Let's try not to worry about it and get some sleep. You have a big day tomorrow."

"Okay, Amiah. Yes, let's try and get some sleep."

I let Amiah take my bed while I laid out an air mattress. My motto was always "A comfortable guest is a happy guest." So I wanted to make sure that Amiah was still comfortable when she was staying with me. It was that way when I was in California too. I tried to fall asleep quickly, but that man kept coming into my head. I wanted the thought of him to go away because I knew it was nothing. It took me until around one-thirty in the morning to finally get some shut-eye. I got about three hours of sleep because I woke up again at four-thirty with my throat dried and needing something to drink. I quietly got up and went downstairs without trying to wake anyone else up in the household. They needed their sleep as well.

When I got downstairs to the kitchen, I got myself a glass of cold water. That usually helped me get to sleep quicker. I took a minute to take in the darkness and calmness of the night. I was going to go on the back patio for a minute, but that was until I swore I saw a shadow in the dark, but it hid behind the bushes after I looked. That scared the living daylights out of me. I went around the house, making sure all the doors and windows were locked. That way, no one could get in easily if there were someone outside. After seeing that I didn't go to sleep for the rest of the night.

Chapter 13

When I got up the next morning, everyone was already up and getting ready for the busy day ahead of us. I took my time getting ready, though, because I still had a feeling that someone was watching me. I had a feeling something terrible was going to happen to my family again, or worse, something was going to happen to me. I didn't dare tell anyone about what I experienced last night. I didn't want to worry them, and then they make me not walk today because they didn't want anything to happen. I had to try my best and put all of that stuff in the back of my mind. I didn't want to think about it. I needed positive thoughts today and not negative ones. Once I got up and dressed in my new dress my parents bought me yesterday I went downstairs to get some breakfast.

Today was one of those breakfast days where we had to get something quick and eat it because, with as many things we had to get done today, we didn't have any time to sit down as a family and eat. Amiah met me downstairs with a brush in her hair and a half-eaten bagel hanging from her mouth. She must have just gotten up a little bit before me, which was unusual because I'm usually always up before her. At least that was how it was in California. Most days, I had to give Amiah a wake-up call so she wouldn't be late for school. After she was done eating her bagel, she tried to hurry up and get her hair done. I forgot that she and I had to go drive to get my grandparents at the airport by eleven-thirty, and it was already eleven. When I noticed the time, I quickly put my hair in a messy bun and brushed my teeth, and I was ready to go. Before I grabbed Amiah to go, she froze.

"What's wrong, Amiah?"

"It's nothing, I just wanted to take this time and enjoy the moment. I know we have a big and special day ahead for you. We need to slow down and remember this day. It is your big graduation day. The four years we have done in high school is coming to an end tonight. In three months, we will be in New York City, living out our dreams of dancing in a big dance school. We have been waiting for this moment for our entire lives."

"Thank you, Amiah, for that realization. I agree. These are the moments that we have been waiting for. Yes, today is about me, but on Monday, it is going to be your big day. You will have finally graduated high school as well. I'm so glad that we can experience these moments together."

"This is so true, Lily. I'm glad that I'll be spending the next four years with my best friend. Let's get going so we can be there on time for your grandparents."

We had to take my sister's car since I didn't have a car yet but would hopefully be getting one here when I get back to California. My sister had a red Camry but couldn't drive it anymore because she lost her driver's license whenever she got taken. I was surprised that my parents, and Maddy, trusted me enough to drive the car since I just got my license a week prior. I was excited, though, to see my grandparents. The airport was about a twenty-minute drive, and so we got there right when my grandparent's flight landed. When I saw them, I ran up and gave them each a hug. The smiles on their faces were the best part of seeing them. I knew they wouldn't admit it, but I was their favorite grandkid. I was spoiled when it came to them.

The whole car ride home, I was telling them about how I got accepted into Juilliard and would be doing their dance program starting in the fall. They knew how Maddy blew her chance at Juilliard and so the topic brought on a serious conversation.

"Lily. This is great news that you got accepted into Juilliard. We both know that you are going to succeed there. You have to promise us one thing, though."

"What would that be, Grammy?"

"You won't be like Maddy and decline this opportunity you have. You have great potential to make it to the top, but you have to want it and actually try."

"I promise I won't make the same mistake as Maddy. Amiah will also be attending Juilliard, and so I will have my best friend there to encourage me and help me through anything that may come my way. I will do the same for her, as well."

"That's great to hear, Lily. We are always a phone call away as well if you are in trouble and need help or just want to talk. It doesn't matter what time of day it is. We will always be available."

"Thank you."

We kept talking about random things all the way home. When I got back, my parents were outside, loading the car up with some of my items. That way we wouldn't be in such a hurry tonight after my graduation. My plane left at midnight. We needed to go straight from my graduation ceremony to the airport. I knew it was going to be a long day. I first helped my grandparents unpack their stuff since they were staying an extra week with my parents and Maddy. After all of their stuff was removed, I went to help my parents. It was the least that I could do since it was my stuff that they were packing. It was an emotional night for me because I was ready for this next chapter of my life. Still, at the same time, I was afraid of being away from my family after everything that had happened recently.

There were definitely tears as I was packing everything into the car. While I was putting all of my dance stuff into the back seat, my dad came up to me and said, "Sweetie, you are going to be at the top of this world one day, and when you are, I'm going to be right there beside you." When he said that, it was like Niagara Falls in my eyes. I gave him a quick hug and a kiss on the check.

"Thanks, Dad. That means a lot. I love you."

"I love you too, princess."

When I looked at the time, I threw my phone into the back seat of the car and rushed to go fix my makeup. It was already five o'clock, and I had to be at the school by five-thirty. Once I fixed my makeup and hair, I grabbed Amiah, and we were out the door. We took Maddy's car, and we zoomed to the school. I think I was going at least fifteen miles over the speed limit just because I needed to get to the school and on time. I was not going to mess this special night up for me or anyone else. I got there with a minute to spare before we went into the auditorium to get in our seats. We had to sit in our seats for a half-hour before families started showing up. I began to get impatient. I wanted to get this night over with so I could finally get on with my life and leave Paris to go back to where I called home. At least for the summer, I would be home, but then starting in the fall, I was going to have to call New York my home.

As I was waiting for the ceremony to start, I kept daydreaming about what Juilliard was going to be like. After visiting the campus, it gave me insight that living on campus for one hundred and eighty days was going to be so much different. I could tell it was going to be a good type of different, but I was still as nervous as could be. Right when I was starting to think about dancing in the big dance studio, my principal came onto the stage to get the ceremony started.

"Good evening Ladies and Gentlemen, to the Class of 1998 Graduating class of Lyceé Janson de Sailly. The moment these students stepped on school grounds as Freshman, or when some of them joined us later in the years, these students made the best out of every situation. They became friends, and eventually, they became a family. No matter what one person was going through, they had an army of friends staying right beside them. They accomplished everything from being President of the National Honor Society to being Captain of the Football Team. We have also had cheer captains and dancers who have shown what they learned throughout the years. They have had tears, but they have also had laughter. I can't personally wait to see and hear what these kids are doing in the upcoming years. Now enough of me going on and on, let's get these kids graduated."

After my principal gave his little speech, he started calling each and every one of us up one by one. I was somewhere in the middle. When I got up on that stage, I looked out in the crowd of people staring at me and couldn't do anything but smile. I saw my mom, dad, sister, Amaih, and my grandparents with the biggest smiles that I have ever seen on any of them. I knew they were proud. When I got back to my seat, I couldn't stop smiling. I didn't think that I was ever going to get to this point in my life, but here I was. A graduated Senior. It took about an hour and a half to get through all of the names. When the last kid got back to their seats, we all exchanged looks like no other. We then all stood up and took our tassels from right to left. Our Alma Mater started playing, and we started going around hugging everyone. Tears were coming down everyone's faces until I realized something terrible.

There was one person in the audience looking straight towards me. It was the same guy that was at our rehearsal yesterday. When I first saw him at the rehearsal, I thought he was looking at someone different, but right then, at the moment, I knew he was looking at me. At that moment, my heart stopped, and I froze. I stood there for five minutes straight. Amiah had to come and knock me out of it.

"Lily. Are you okay?"

"I don't know."

Chapter 14

The whole way to the airport I was silent. The image of the guy kept running through my head like the water in the sunlight. I was getting more anxious as I was getting closer to the airport. I knew as soon as I got on the plane and got to California, I would be safe. At least that is what I was hoping would happen. My mind was in the gutter, I didn't realize we were already at the airport for the past fifteen minutes, and my parents were busy unloading the car. When I came to the realization, I slowly got out of the car and started loading all of my stuff back into the car. My parents gave each other this confused look. Amiah quickly got back in the car with me. I didn't give her a second even to ask me a question before I spilled everything that I was feeling out to her.

"I saw that same guy today, Amiah. Tonight was different, though. I knew he was looking straight at me. His face was red, and it looked like he wanted to get revenge on me for doing something terrible to him. The only thing is I don't know who the guy is. I feel like he is after me. I'm afraid that after I leave, he is going to go after my family or something after everything that has happened, I can't take that chance. I need to stay here. I need to protect my family."

"Lily. I know how you are feeling. I noticed that man too, but I think you are overreacting to all of this. I honestly think he had a kid that was in your class, and you didn't know it. Our plane leaves in an hour and half, and as soon as we get on that plane to head home, your qualms will be gone, and we won't have to worry. We can take the summer to do all the things we used to do before you moved. The weather will be nice, so we can go to drive-in movies, grab an ice cream and take a hike in the woods by my house, and there is a certain guy that has missed you and is waiting patiently to see you again."

"You are right, Amiah. Thank you. Who is this guy that is waiting for me?"

"Does the name Lucien Raley sound familiar?"

When I heard that name, the next thing I remembered was hitting my head on the car door. Lucien Raley was my first crush, and dare I say, my first love. When I was in California, he was one of the popular guys, but before high school we dated for two years. When we entered high school, Lucien wanted nothing to do with me because he didn't want to ruin his reputation. He never showed interest in me after that, and so I don't know what changed his mind in the last three years.

"What name did you say, Amiah?"

"Lucien Raley."

"There is no way that hottie Lucien Raley is back in California waiting for me."

"Well, believe it, Lily. I was texting him the other night, and he was saying how excited he was about you coming back home for the summer. He was also saying how he made the mistake of not asking you out before you left for France."

"You know I don't believe you, Amiah, but I guess I will have to wait and see what happens whenever we get to California. Now let's get out of this car and get our stuff so we can get to California."

"That's my girl. I knew you would change your mind."

When I knew that I was doing the right thing, I got out of the car and grabbed all my stuff and headed back towards the airport doors once more. My family followed behind me with red faces and tears streaming down their faces. I could tell that they didn't want me to leave, but I knew that I had to so I could be independent and do what I could to achieve my dreams with my best friend by my side.

Once I got to where I had to start going through security, I turned to my family, and even though they weren't crying and always had smiles on their faces, I knew deep down they were hurting. The pain would soon go away once they knew I was safe and landed in California. I gave them one last hug, and Amiah and I were off.

As we were boarding the plane, Amiah looked over to me and gave me this sly smile like she had something planned but didn't want me to know about it.

"What do you think, Amiah?"

"Do you want to know?"

"Yes. I want to know what you are thinking. You only have that smile when you are up to no good."

"Okay. I'm thinking about how awesome it would be if you and Lucien got together. You would be all over the town. The headlines would be called 'Mr. Popular with Juilliard Bound Dancer.'"

"I truly doubt we would make headlines, but it would be awesome if he asked us out. I guess we will just have to wait and see what happens."

"I guess we will. Let's just enjoy this plane ride as we imagine everything that can happen once we land. Deal?"

"Deal."

We hugged and then found our seats and got comfy. We had a portable DVD player, and so I got that out and put our favorite movie 'The Notebook' in so we could hopefully make the time go faster. After a couple of hours of flying, I fell asleep and had a peaceful dream. The dream was about Lucian and me.

Lucien had picked me up from my house one evening and had an evening full of activities for us to do. We first went to this fancy restaurant that was a couple of blocks from his house. This restaurant was Chez Panisse. It was one of the most elegant restaurants in all of California. I always wanted to go there, but the prices were outrageous. It was almost a hundred dollars for one person, and that wasn't including drinks either. I couldn't believe that Lucien could afford this place, especially since his family lost a lot of wealth after his dad got in an accident and got killed. His dad was one of the best-known surgeons in all of California, and so he brought in most of the family's income.

While we were eating dinner, this group of violinists came into the dining area and started playing romantic music. They had a little space where people could dance if they wanted and so Lucien grabbed my hand and led me to the dance floor. We danced to the song 'All About Us' by Owl City. It was such a romantic time that right before the song ended, Lucien and I had our first kiss. His lips were as soft as ice cream that has been sitting out in the sun for a few minutes. After we got done with dinner, he took me to the beach for horseback riding. The sun was setting in the background, which made it even more romantic. The ride lasted about a half-hour.

After we got done with the trip, Lucien took me back to his place. It was midnight, and so I couldn't go back to my house that late. When we got back to his house, we both went to bed with me on the couch and him in his room. That is the part when I woke up from Amiah, gently shaking me to get up.

"Lily. We landed in California. It's time to get up."

"We are here already? That was quick."

"Maybe that is because you slept most of the way, but yes, we are here."

"Okay."

I grabbed all of my bags from the overhead compartment and helped Amiah with a bunch of her stuff. We slowly walked off the bus as I was still trying to wake up from my restful sleep. When we walked into the airport, I didn't realize it at first, but there was this tall, blond-haired, blue-eyed, hottie figure standing in front of us with a sign saying *Welcome home Lily. I know you just got home, but will you be my special girl and be mine?*

At first, I didn't read that right and thought the sign said Amiah, but after a few seconds, I rubbed my eyes and saw that it said Lily and I fainted. Lucien was right there asking me to be his girlfriend, and I passed out.

Lucien came over to try and help me up. When I opened my eyes, Lucien was over the top of me, staring with his bright pretty blue eyes.

"Lucien. Is that you?"

"Yes, beautiful, it is me."

"What are you doing here?"

"What do you think, Lily? I am here to claim you as mine, and I hope you will say yes. I know this is out of the blue, but after you left, I realized that I made a mistake of not asking you out before. What do you say? Will you be mine?"

"Maybe this will answer your question." I got up and kissed him on those beautiful lips. He helped me up and held me close. I looked at Amiah, who was all smiles and giggles.

"You knew about this the entire time, didn't you?"

"Possibly. Lucien didn't want me to tell you. He wanted to surprise you. I hope you aren't mad at me."

"Mad at you? No way. I could never be mad at you. I owe you a huge thank you. Now come here."

I gave Amiah a huge hug. "If it weren't for you, Amiah, I would still be in France fearing for my life. Instead, I am here with my boyfriend, thinking of how this is going to be the best summer yet."

"You are welcome, Lily. I knew I needed to get you back to California where you belong. Now I think that you and Lucien have some catching up to do so I will let you two be. I will take your stuff to the house and will see you tonight."

"Okay. Thank you, Amiah."

I looked at Lucien, and he gave me another kiss and grabbed my hand. In my mind, I knew that this was going to be a great summer.

Chapter 15

On the whole way to Lucien's house, he was telling me that ever since I left, his whole life has changed. He said that his mom had remarried, and his stepdad is a traveler for his job and gets to go on all of these trips to research books that authors want him to do. While he was telling me all about his life and the new family, I kept thinking of how much in love I was with him. Everything he said had this tone and expression that just went straight to my heart and was telling me that this new relationship could work out as I was listening. However, something didn't make any sense. He said that his stepdad was usually only gone for a week or two, but this trip, he had been gone for three months and was somewhere near Paris.

When we got back to his house, he came around and helped me out of the car. He was, for sure, a gentleman. Nothing had changed about him. Once we got into the house, his little sister came running up to me because before I left, I usually babysat her after school for a couple of hours. Her name was Valeryia. She was adopted by the Raley family when she was only two weeks old. Lucien and his family were living in Ukraine for a couple of years, and right before they came and moved to California, they decided to adopt a baby. She was now eight years old. Valeryia has changed a lot since the last time I saw her. I picked her up in my arms and twirled her around like the princess she was. She had this cutest laugh that was contagious. After I put her down, Lucien took me by the hand, and we went out to his back yard where he had a hammock set up. We went and laid down while trying to catch up on life and what we had planned for the summer.

Once I told him that I was going to be attending Juilliard for their dancing team, he insisted on me dancing for him. He put on some ballet music without words, and I did one of my routines that reminded me of Mrs. Marine. The routine had the only Arabesque move. It is a position supported on one leg, which can be straight or in a demi-plie, with the other leg extended behind and at right angles to it. The arms are held in various positions creating the most extended possible lines from the fingertips outward. When I ended in the finishing position, Lucien came over and kissed me passionately. His little sister came out right when he did, and she grabbed me by the arm and dragged me to her room.

"What is going on, Valeryia? Why did you do this?"

She didn't answer me at first. She just had tears coming down her face. She showed me a text, and at first, I didn't want to believe what the text said. The message read:

Lily better be careful, or what I did to you, I will do to her, but she won't make it out alive.

When I read that, I thought Valeryia was just messing around and trying to scare me like she used to. I sat her down and had a serious talk with her.

"Valeryia. Don't scare me like this again. It isn't funny, and it is a serious matter. I have had a lot going on ever since I left, and I don't need any more drama added on to my life. I know you have missed me and want to catch up, but this wasn't the way to do it. Do you understand?"

"I understand, Lily. It's not a joke. I'm serious. My dad sent this text to me." Tears started running down her face even harder than before. I re-read the text to see if there was some way I could tell this wasn't a joke. Before I had the chance to read the text, Valeryia pulled down her pants and showed me both of her legs, which had bruises. When I asked her how she got those, she could only point to the text.

"Does Lucien and your mom know about this, Valeryia?"

"No. He told me that if anyone found out that I would be dead in an instance and so I have always kept it to myself. Please don't tell them. I don't want to die."

"We have to tell someone, and I will make sure that no one can get to you."

"Lily. No!"

Valeryia threw a temper tantrum and clamped on to my legs so I couldn't move. Lucien came up when he heard her screaming.

"What in the world is going on here?"

Before I could answer, Valeryia yelled in his face saying nothing. He then took me by the hand into his room to get the full story out.

"Lily. What is going on?"

"Want the truth?"

"Always."

"Okay, here goes nothing. Valeryia pulled me into her room. She showed me a text that your stepdad supposedly sent to her, saying, 'Lily better be careful or what I did to you I will do to her, but she won't make it out alive.' I thought that this was something Valeryia was making up because she thought it would be funny, but then she showed me bruises on her legs, and now I don't know what to believe."

"Oh, wow. Let me tell my mom, and you go in there with Valeryia and let her know that everything is going to be okay. I know how she hates commotion and how she always thinks that she did something wrong."

"Will do."

When I entered Valeryia's room, she was on her bed with her head in her pillow and crying. She mumbled something, but I couldn't understand what she said. I went over to her and gently rubbed her back, trying to calm her down. In my mind, I thought about what kind of monster entered this family and also who would want to hurt such a beautiful princess like Valeryia. She would do anything to see someone else smile. That is why she couldn't stay mad at me forever for telling someone about what had happened to her.

Eventually, she stopped crying and hugged me. She whispered into my ear, "Thank you for helping me tell someone. I was afraid of telling Lucien."

I smiled, gave her a little kiss on the forehead, and said, "You're welcome—anything for a princess."

Right then, Lucien and his mother came storming in the room. Lucien's mother grabbed Valeryia and rushed her straight to the car. Lucien said that they were going to take her to the hospital. I told them that I was going to go with them so I could be right by her side through everything.

Lucien and I drove separately from his mom and sister so we could have a little bit more alone time since we got interrupted. I finally felt comfortable to tell Lucien about the mysterious person that has been following me. When he heard that he immediately pulled over to the side of the road.

"Lily. Why didn't you tell me about this sooner?"

"I didn't think that it would matter that much, especially now since I am here in California. Why are you freaking out so much?"

"I don't want to see anything bad happen to you, either, Lily."

"Nothing is going to happen to me, Lucien. I am fine. Thank you for worrying, but I have it all under control."

"Okay, Lily. I believe you."

"Good. Now let's hurry up and get to the hospital with your sister."

"Okay."

The rest of the drive to the hospital was silent. It was bringing up memories of when I was on my way to the hospital to see Mrs. Marine. Instead of showing tears, though, I kept looking to Lucien to see how he was doing. I can't imagine what he was feeling through this all. First, his dad got killed. Second, his mom got remarried, and then the person that was supposed to protect the family hurt it instead. Every time I looked over there, he was smiling and had this lovely stare in his eyes. I couldn't believe I was so lucky to have been given a chance to be with him.

When we got to the hospital, I was the first one to get to Valeryia. According to the doctors, when they got into the room, all she wanted was me. I went over to her, and her little brown eyes were still red, but she was smiling at me. She didn't say anything, but she handed me a picture. It was a picture of the same guy who was watching me while I was in Paris.

"Who is this, Valeryia?"

"My stepdad. I never get rid of the picture since I never know when I might truly need it."

When I heard that, I threw the picture on the ground and ran out of the room. Lucien came running after me.

"What is wrong, Lily?"

"That picture your sister handed me is a picture of the man that was following me and stalking me while I was in Paris."

"Are you sure?"

"I'm positive. I wouldn't lie to you."

"I don't know, Lily. I just don't know if you have the right guy."

"I do, Lucien! I don't know why you wouldn't believe me in a situation like this!"

I was so furious with Lucien that I called Amiah to come to get me from the hospital. She only lived a block away from the hospital, so it only took her three minutes to get to me. Once I was in the car, I broke down crying. All the feelings that I felt back in Paris were coming back to me. I told Amiah how I figured out who my stalker was.

"Lily. I can't believe your boyfriend's stepdad is the one that is after you."

"I know, but with this said, I have to be extra careful now because we never know if he will find me again."

"This is true. From now on, if you ever need to go out and do anything, I have to be with you. I don't want anything bad to happen to you. Your parents like me too much, and I can't bear to tell them that something bad happened to you because I was careless and let you go out when I knew you could be in danger."

"Amiah. I don't need a babysitter. I am seventeen years old and can look out for myself. I appreciate what you are trying to do, and I promise if I feel like I am in danger in any way, I will tell you. Does that sound okay?"

"Okay, Lily. I trust you. You are my best friend, and I don't want to see anything bad happen to you or worse I don't want to lose you."

"Thank you, Amiah. I appreciate that much more than you know."

"Anything for you, Lily."

For the next couple of months, I stayed close to Amiah and kept my head up high. Whoever was watching me knew how to stay undercover. Every time I would see him, he would be with another person each time. I warned Amiah whenever I would see him. She made sure I was safe and with her no matter what she had to do. If only the police had been able to find him it would have set my mind at ease.

Chapter 16

The summer went by fast. I spent a lot of time with Lucien. We made up and continued to grow our relationship. The night before I left for Juilliard, he did something that I wasn't expecting at all. He gave me a night to remember.

It was a rainy evening, so we couldn't do what we usually did on Sunday nights, and that was going to the drive-in movies. Instead, he decided that we could still do movies, but we could do it at his house. His mother wasn't home, and so we had to watch Valeryia. It was cool because she went to bed early. After all, she always got headaches when it rained, and so on those nights she would be in bed by eight.

When we put her to bed, we went up to his room to watch a movie. We chose the movie 'The Notebook' by Nicholas Sparks. It was one of my all-time favorite movies. I'm surprised he agreed to watch it because he usually didn't like movies like that, but because I was leaving the next day, he wanted to make sure I had the most fantastic night of my life.

In the middle of the movie, though, he didn't want to watch the film anymore. When I wasn't paying attention, I felt the coolness of his skin drag up my legs and his arms around my body. I then felt his hot breath on my neck. My body tingled, and I turned over to face him, and his lips were as close to mine as his body was. I knew at the moment what he wanted, but I didn't want the same thing. I kissed him gently on the lips and then got up to go to check on Valeryia. He didn't like that because when I got back to the room, he grabbed me and pushed me on the bed.

"Lily. What is up with you tonight? I am trying to make this a night that you won't forget. Why won't you let me do this for you?"

"Lucien. I don't want this. You know how I feel about the situation. Why won't you respect my decision? I thought you were a gentleman."

"I am a gentleman, but I am going to get what you want!"

"Not tonight, you aren't!"

I grabbed all of my stuff and ran out of his house as fast as a cheetah. When I came rushing into Amiah's house, I quickly locked all the doors so Lucien couldn't get in.

"What is going on, Lily?" Amiah questioned.

"Lucien tried to have sex with me, and when I told him no, he got aggressive. I'm not going to have that. Especially not before we leave for Juilliard tomorrow. I need to focus on everything that I am about to encounter."

"That monster! I can't believe he would try to do something like this to you. I thought he cared and loved you."

"I thought he did too, but I guess we were both wrong. I loved him but not that much to let him take something so precious when I knew we were probably not going to last. He and I are over. He ruined this relationship."

"Good, Lily. I am proud of you for standing up for what you believe and not letting him pressure you into doing something that you aren't comfortable doing."

"I am stronger than what he thinks I am. I am going to text him right now and tell him that we are through."

"You go, Lily!"

As soon as I got up to my room, I texted him. What he had to say next was not pleasant.

Lucien. We're over. What you just tried to pull a couple of minutes ago was the line, and you crossed it. I can't afford to do something that I might regret later. I am leaving for Juilliard first thing in the morning and wanted to make sure that you knew we were not together. I don't want to hear from you again. Thank you for an amazing summer and loving me, but I am sorry.

Lily. We aren't done. I want to be together and I always get what I want. You are stubborn, and I don't like that you are this way.

If you don't like it, then why do you want to continue to be with me anyway?

I want you to be mine.

Well, too bad. Goodbye.

As soon as I sent that text, I blocked his number and deleted everything that reminded me of him or us. I couldn't believe in three short months I got in a relationship, and then I left the most amazing guy. I knew that there were going to be many other guys, but Lucien was the one I don't think I was ever going to forget. I had to try my best and get him out of my mind. I needed to get sleep because Amiah and I had to be at the airport at three in the morning to catch our flight.

That night I tried my hardest to fall asleep, but for some reason, Lucien was on my mind the whole night. There were times that I thought about picking up the phone and calling him to apologize and see if he would take me back, but the more I honestly thought about it, I knew deep down in my heart that it wouldn't be a good idea. I tried to put some jazz music on since that usually helped, but tonight was different. Nothing that I was trying seemed to help me. I tried counting sheep, and I think that is what made me bored out of my mind and knocked me out. I slept for a good two hours before Amiah woke me up and told me that it was time to get up.

It took me about twenty minutes to get up and moving. I wanted to sleep just a little bit longer. Two hours was not enough sleep. Once I got up and running, my phone was going off again. I didn't recognize the number, and so I didn't answer it. After about twenty minutes of getting calls from this same number, I finally decided to solve it. I didn't like who was on the other end.

"Lily. I want to apologize. I can promise that I won't ever hurt you again. I need you in my life. If you leave I am going to be heartbroken. Please don't go to Juilliard."

"Too bad, Lucien. We are not getting back together and I am leaving for Juilliard. There is nothing you can say or do that will stop me from doing what I need to, so I can achieve my dreams."

"Whatever you say, Lily. So that you know you are making a huge mistake."

"No, I am not. Once I get on that plane I am not going to look back. I will admit that I had a great summer but I can forget about it and will forget about it. I have the future to look forward to, and I can't wait to see what it has in hold for me. Lucien, goodbye."

I hung up after that and continued packing. We needed to hurry up so Lucien couldn't get in contact with me anymore. I was fed up with him and all his tricks to make me try to give up my dream. I wondered if that was his whole aim this whole summer was to make me feel like I actually was loved and was worth something but if that was his plan then it failed epically. I was an independent young lady who didn't need a man in my life.

Amiah and I got done packing within a half-hour, and it was time for us to say goodbye to her family. It was one of those moments that not just one of us was crying, but everyone in the room was crying. They were like a second family to me and helped me with so much that I hated to leave them, but I was doing what I wanted.

On the way to the airport, Amiah and I kept looking at each other with worried looks. We didn't know what to expect on the way to Juilliard. We didn't know what would happen once we got there. We knew that we had an apartment ready for us, but we were two teenagers doing something like no other. We were going into the big city with no money, no idea what we were doing, and terrified out of our minds. The plane ride was calming. Amiah and I did our own things through the whole duration of the trip. Once we stepped off the plane we were introduced to warm weather, green trees everywhere, people coming up to us to talk, and the smell of corn dogs and hamburgers. We didn't know what we were to expect, but we were ready for the adventure that we had ahead of us.

Chapter 17

Our apartment was only a five-minute walk from the airport. We decided though since we had so much luggage to call a taxi to take us there just for this one time. Our apartment was huge. It was a red brick building with white shingles, blue curtains, and a vegetable garden on the right side of the building. It took us about ten minutes to unload all of our stuff from the taxi into our apartment. For a two minute drive time and a ten minute unloading time, it cost us thirty dollars for everything. It was ridiculous, but I guess that was what we should have expected before moving to New York. Everything here was high in price and ridiculous. We started to unpack everything. It wasn't even fifteen minutes before we heard a knock on the door.

"Who could it be? We just got here, and I doubt that anyone truly knows we are here already?"

"I don't know, but let's answer it. I'll come with you."

We quietly walked to the door and looked through the peephole. It was an older gentleman with a suit jacket and a nice tie. We put the chain lock on, but we could still open the door a little, so we could at least talk to the person, but they couldn't get in.

"Hello?"

"Hi. I'm looking for Lily and Amiah."

"Who are you," I shyly asked before giving the strange man a definite answer.

"Let me introduce myself. My name is Louie Blank. I am the landlord of this building and just needed some papers signed."

"Okay. Well, I am Lily, and this is Amiah."

We opened the door so we could retrieve the papers that we needed to fill out and sign.

"I will need these papers back by the end of the week, please."

"Will do, Mr. Blank. Thank you."

Amiah set the papers in her purse since we didn't have anywhere to put them yet. Mrs. Bean sent us an email a couple of days prior, saying that the college would deliver us furniture at five o'clock the night that we arrived. It took a little longer than expected to get our furniture because by seven o'clock the furniture wasn't there yet. So Amiah and I decided to go and try to find something to eat so we didn't have to wait all night to grab something to eat. We knew from previous knowledge that unless you knew New York like the back of your hand, then it is probably a good idea not to go out past nine at night.

After about ten minutes of walking, we found this little restaurant a mile past Juilliard. The menu was up on the window outside with prices, and they were reasonable. Since we still had a hundred dollars to last until we started school in two days, we thought it would be a good idea to eat cheap so we could save money in case some sort of emergency came up.

The restaurant was small outside but huge inside. It was like a tavern where there was a bar but also a separate area for people who didn't drink or just wanted to have a nice meal without it being as loud. Amiah and I didn't drink, so we decided to sit in the diner portion. We found a booth that was red with smooth brown leather seats. When we took a closer look at the menu we found a meal that we both wanted without taking much time to think about it. They had Chicken

Marsala. My mom used to make it for us every Thursday night after school. My grandma had a secret recipe for it and she would only tell one person in the family right before she died. It was a tradition. It went all the way back to my great-great-great-great-great-grandmother. I'm surprised my grandma chose my mom to get the recipe. It was the one thing that I always looked forward to, and after I introduced Amiah to it, she was obsessed. We ordered that and got a side of onion rings. We talked and laughed about times when we messed up on dancing, but it was funny how we did it. I went first.

We were at a rehearsal for a play in fifth grade. I was one of the lead dancers, and I had a difficult task of twirling five times and then landing in a chair on my last twirl. I practiced it like crazy at home, school, and in the park sometimes. I thought I had it down perfect, so when it came to the actual opening night, then I wouldn't mess up. Well, right before opening night we had a two-hour rehearsal. When it came down to me doing that part I had a rough start but got better after my third spin but then ended badly. Right when I twirled and sat on the seat, I fell out of the chair, and my friend Andrew caught me right before I hit my head on the floor. He was one of the cutest guys in the play but after fifth grade, his parents moved him all the way to Florida so he could go to a private school for piano players. I haven't heard from him since.

Amiah and I laughed so much we didn't even notice that our food was there already. We ate while Amiah told me a story of how she and her brother were in a forest riding dirt bikes. She went early in the morning to create an obstacle course for them to drive through. She found some old parts of an old building that used to be in the wood and so she used that to make a ramp that they were to drive up and try to do a flip through the air while still staying on the dirt bike. Amiah used to do tricks on the dirt bike whenever she wasn't dancing, which wasn't often. Her brother is the one that got her interested in that type of thing. After she completed making the obstacle course she tested it, to make sure it was safe. She got through it safely and then went to get her brother. They spent all day going through the course and adding to it. Around nine-thirty that night, it was time to go home, but Amiah wanted to do the course one more time. When she was going through the path, she went over the first ramp and then was going to go over the second one. Right when she got to the edge of the slope, and the front of the dirt bike went flying, she tried to do the flip. Still, instead of staying on the bike, she flipped off and ended up going over a tree branch and catching it right before she fell to the ground. Her brother Davie helped her down off the tree. We laughed our butts off after she finished her story. By the time she finished, we had finished our food, and it was nine at night. We needed to head back to the place since our furniture was supposed to be there already.

We quickly walked back to the house because it was dark and getting to be creepy outside. It was loud, though, but there was no such thing as a quiet night in New York. When we got to our apartment, we saw Mrs. Bean standing outside on the stairs.

"Hi, Mrs. Bean. How are you?"

"Girls! I'm so happy to see you guys."

"You are?"

"Yes, I am."

"Why is that?"

"I just wasn't sure if you guys made it safely or not. I thought I would come to check on you guys, and when I got here, you weren't here, and so I thought something bad happened to you."

"Oh no, we are okay. We went out to eat since our furniture wasn't available when we got here around three this afternoon. After we unpacked everything around seven or so, we decided we didn't want to wait any longer to get food, so we went to this restaurant about a mile down the road."

"Okay. I am glad you guys explained that. It looks like your furniture is here now so I will let you girls get some sleep. You guys should take the time tomorrow to explore the city since starting on Monday you have to be at the school first thing in the morning. There are so many things you guys can do on a Sunday in New York. For example, many local musicians play in Times Square, museums are open, and then there are parks that you can walk around in and explore."

"Thanks, Mrs. Bean. We will see you on Monday."

"Sounds good. Good night, girls."

"Good night, Mrs. Bean."

Once she left, Amiah and I went back inside, and Mrs. Bean was right, our furniture did arrive and was all in the center of the room. There was just one thing that didn't seem right. That was how in the world did the people that brought the furniture get into our apartment. We are the only ones that have keys unless Mr. Blank let them in. That was a possibility as well. We let it slip out of our minds though just because we were so tired that we wanted and needed to get some sleep. When we were finally ready for bed it was almost midnight already. Our beds weren't available, yet, so we just dug through our stuff for our sleeping bags and made ourselves comfortable on the living room floor. It was so cold in the living room that it took us to digging out three more blankets before we could genuinely be warm. I could tell that it was going to be a long night.

My prediction came true when it was around three in the morning. I felt like someone was watching us, but I knew it was impossible. I got up, though, and walked through the whole house just to make sure. I doubled checked the front door, the back patio door, all the windows, and I even checked the vent. It was possible someone could have climbed up into the flue from another apartment and crawled to us. After reviewing and securing everything, I went back to try and get some more sleep, but I still felt like something was off. I didn't know what it was, but I knew it was something. I wasn't going to be able to sleep until I figured out what it was.

Over the next two hours, I swore I kept hearing knocking at the door and windows, but whenever I would get up to check, there was nothing nor anyone there. The very last time that I got up, I must have made a lot of noise because I accidentally woke Amiah up.

"What in the world are you doing, Lily? It is five in the morning. The birds aren't even up yet, and so that means we shouldn't either."

"I'm sorry, Amiah. I couldn't sleep at all these past two hours. I thought I kept hearing noises, but I haven't figured out what is causing them."

"It's probably nothing, Lily. Now try to go to sleep. We are going to be getting up in three hours for the day, and you need some kind of sleep."

"Okay, Amiah, I will try."

Right after that, I fell asleep right away. I don't know what was different, but whatever it was, I liked it. I slept like a baby.

Eight o'clock rolled around quickly. I didn't want to get up, but I got woken up by the aroma of pancakes, sausage, and bacon. Amiah woke up early and went to go find us something to eat before we got started with the day. Once I got up and at least dressed we both sat down to eat together and discuss what we wanted to do on our one free day before classes. We could do anything we wanted, we just promised each other that no matter what we would both stick together so nothing would happen to us. After about ten minutes we decided we would go to Times Square and do some shopping around to get some things we needed and wanted for the apartment, then we would go to the park to walk around, and then to end the day we would come back here to get some dancing in so we could freshen up on our dance moves. We didn't want to mess up on simple things in class on our first day. That would not look good for either of us.

Once breakfast was done and cleaned up, we took the next half hour to shower up and get ready. I turned on some dancing music, and we were off doing our things. We didn't care what kind of dancing we did while getting prepared as long as we didn't distract each other. About ten minutes into everything there was a knock on our door. When I went to answer it, it was a young gentleman that lived above us. He didn't look happy with us. Our music was too loud because it woke his one-year-old daughter up.

"Hi. I don't know you, but please keep your music down! I will only tell you this once. If I have to come down here again at any time during the duration of you living here I will go to Mr. Blank. I am not playing. You are not the only person living in this apartment."

"We are sorry. We didn't realize the music was that loud. It will not happen again."

"Good!"

The man walked away angrily, while mumbling something under his breath. I couldn't believe the attitude that he had. We honestly didn't know that our music was that loud. He could have quickly just told us it was a bit too noisy, and then we would have turned it down. When I shut the door, I went back to Amiah to tell her what just happened.

"Are you serious, Lily? Our music isn't that loud. It is loud enough for us to hear while getting ready."

"I know. I think he was just having a bad morning and needed someone to take it out on, and our neighbor chose us since he knew we are new."

"Possibly. Oh well. Let's just forget it and continue getting ready. I want to get to some of these shops before it's too late into the afternoon. I know how busy they can get."

"Okay, Amiah."

We finally got done getting ready around ten and were ready to go. We were just about out the door when all of a sudden, we turned to the window to check everything, and there was a strange figure standing at the window looking in and staring at us. We yelled, and it scared whoever or whatever it was away. We had no idea what in the world just happened. We were nervous about leaving the apartment now, but we couldn't let fear keep us from doing what we wanted to do. We regretted leaving after about fifteen minutes of walking.

Chapter 18

We kept hearing footsteps that weren't ours the whole way to Times Square, but whenever we would look behind us we wouldn't see anybody. We thought that if we put headphones in then it would go away. We were correct for about another five minutes, but then the footsteps came back. After the fifth time looking back, we did see a young couple walking. Still, we didn't think that it was them because they were a couple of hundred feet away from us, and the footsteps that we were hearing were closer like maybe ten or fifteen feet behind us.

We quickly got to Times Square and found a shop that looked interesting. When we got into the shop, the footsteps stopped again the whole time we were shopping. Amiah and I were afraid to walk back out into the street. We had a weird feeling that something was going to happen. I came up with the idea of telling someone, so maybe they could help us out. I found a store associate that looked like she could be helpful. I ran up to her in a panic, and she quickly spun around to face me.

"Hi. Are you okay? What is going on?"

"Hi. My name is Lily, and this is Amiah. I know this may sound strange, but we need your help. We are new to New York and just moved into an apartment. Ever since last night, we have had this strange feeling that someone has been watching and following us. This morning we saw someone staring into our window, but when we yelled it scared them off. Now, when we were on our way here, we swore we heard footsteps right behind us. We are terrified to walk out of here. Can you help us?"

"Yes, I will help you guys. Wait right here. I will get our Officer that patrols the store. We can help you guys."

"Okay, great! Thank you," I paused for a minute, not knowing her name.

"My name is Marilyn Gonzalez."

"Thank you, Marilyn."

"No problem. Now, wait here."

"Okay."

As we were waiting for Marilyn, Amiah and I were looking all around us to make sure that no one was following us. What a great way to start our first full day in New York. Right as we were waiting, I got a phone call. The caller id said that it was from my sister Maddy. I quickly answered it, so she didn't think that there was anything wrong.

"Hi, Maddy. How are you? What's new?"

"Nothing much but wanted to warn you that there is someone in New York that is kidnapping young ladies. He kidnaps them and, after holding them for a year, kills them. It was just on the news today that they found a young lady in an old abandoned church. The same kind of event happened a year ago as well. It is the same person. He just waits a year until his next victim. I guess what I'm trying to say is be careful. I don't want anything happening to you."

"Thanks, Maddy. I'll be careful. Amiah and I never leave each other's side for that reason because we don't want anything bad happening to each other."

"Okay. Good. I am glad to hear that. Mom and Dad have been worried sick about you. You haven't answered any of their phone calls. What is up with that?"

"Tell them I'm sorry. I've just been busy with unpacking everything and getting used to the city. Amiah and I are taking today to explore the city. Tell them that I will call them tonight before I go to bed."

"Okay, Lily. Thank you. I love you. Have fun today and be safe."

"Will do. Bye, Maddy."

When I got off the phone, Marilyn came around the corner with a police officer.

"Hi. You must be Lily and Amiah. I am Officer Jose. Marilyn here told me that you guys were coming into some strange events ever since you guys arrived here in New York yesterday. Is that correct?"

"Yes, it is. We keep feeling that someone is watching us and following us. We can't seem to get away from the feeling no matter what we do."

"Okay. Well, we have a few options that we could do for you girls. The first option is we can put you guys in a hotel and have you stay hidden for a couple of days. Another option is we can have a patrol car stay outside of your residence for a couple of days in case something were to happen. We would be right there to help."

"Amiah and I start classes tomorrow at Juilliard, so is there any way that we could stay at our house and then get a ride to Juilliard. That way, we don't have to walk and have no one following us."

"We can arrange for that to happen. Was there anything else you girls wanted to do this morning?"

Amiah and I exchanged looks, and we both reluctantly agreed that we would go back to the house and stay hidden for the day until classes in the morning. Officer Jose gave us a lift home and then dispatched a couple of his day shift officers to come out in front of the apartment building. We had to let Mr. Blank know, that way he didn't think something all that bad was happening in his building, and it was all for the safety of two of his tenants. Mr. Blank was surprisingly all okay about it. In fact, he was more than okay. He told us that if we ever felt in any kind of danger to go to him right away and he will do everything in his power to make sure we are safe, and nothing happens to us. I thought what he said was one of the most helpful things he had spoken to us within the last day and a half that we had been there. He didn't truly make an excellent first impression on us, but now I had a feeling that he was actually a really cool guy.

The next couple of hours went really slow. Still, I think it was just because Amiah and I were stuck in the house because we didn't want the police to work even harder than they already had to, that way nothing went wrong. I couldn't believe the luck Amiah and I were having. Within the first two days, before classes started, we had the police on our radar because of our subconscious. Every time I looked out the window I jumped a little each time because I kept forgetting that there were police there and that they were going to stay there for at least a week they said. Obviously, it wasn't going to be the same set of police officers during the day, but there would always be at least two.

That night neither Amiah nor I could fall asleep. We knew we needed to because the next day was going to be longer than the day before. We tried everything we could until we decided to get up and dance until we fell asleep. We had a good idea because it only took another five minutes for us to get so tired that we landed on the ground and stayed there until morning.

We had such a peaceful sleep after we did get some shut-eye. I decided to get up early and go get some breakfast for Amiah and me as well as the police officers that have stayed up all night just for our protection. It was the least I could do for them. The only problem was if I knew what was going to happen as soon as I stepped out of my front door, I would have made a better choice.

Chapter 19

I got about a mile down the road before I had the feeling that someone was following me again. I knew I shouldn't have been worried since the police knew where I was going. However, it was still the anxiety I'd had about the past couple of days. The feeling went away though after about fifteen minutes of walking. Once I got to the bakery, I quickly got a dozen doughnuts and got out of there so I could hurry up and get home.

The walk home was peaceful up until the last three minutes. I had my headphones in and wasn't paying any attention when all of a sudden, I got bumped. I got so scared that I dropped all of the doughnuts.

"I'm so sorry. I didn't even see you there. Are you okay?"

I didn't answer him as I caught myself looking into his dreamy eyes.

"Ma'am."

"Hi. Yes, I am okay except that I dropped my breakfast."

"Again, I'm sorry. I had my music on, and when I go for my morning runs, I tend not to pay attention to my surroundings. Here, let me help you with that."

As I helped get the box of doughnuts, I couldn't help but catch his eyes again.

"My name is Matthias Law, by the way."

"Nice to meet you, Matthias. I'm Lily."

"Nice to meet you as well, Lily. Here are your doughnuts. They don't look bad, just a little shaken."

"Thank you. Well, I better get going. I have a long day ahead of me."

"Wait. What's the rush? Let me buy you a coffee to make up for running into you."

"I can't. I'm sorry. I got to go."

"Oh, come on. Don't be a goody-two-shoes."

"I said no! Thank you for offering, but I got to go."

"You are going to regret telling me no, Lily."

"Whatever," I grabbed the doughnuts, held them to my chest, and ran home as fast as I could.

Once I got home, I gave the police officers their doughnuts, but I didn't tell them about the incident that happened. I didn't want them to work more than they were already. Once I got inside the house, there was a note left by Amiah.

Lily. I got up and didn't know where you went, but the police told me, and then I decided to take a quick twenty minute run around the block. I should be back by the time you get home, but if I do not get back before you, just start getting ready. When I get home, we will only have a limited time to get to class. I can't wait for this next chapter in our lives.

I listened to what Amiah said and got ready. After about five minutes, I heard a knock on the door. I thought it was Amiah, and she just forgot her key when she left. When I opened the door, it was not Amiah. Right in front of me was a tall figure, all dressed in black.

In a matter of seconds, I had a bag over my head, was blindfolded, and got carried away. I tried screaming and kicking, but whoever had a hold of me covered my mouth so no one could hear me. I was soon out cold because I couldn't breathe well. I got woken up after I got thrown into what seemed like the back of a car or a trunk. I tried kicking the door and window with my feet to try and see if I could break something, but I had no luck. The more I struggled, the more the person punished me by slapping me extremely hard. It took about five slappings before I learned my lesson, and I just shut my mouth. After a long and bumpy ride, we finally stopped somewhere. I heard the car door open and was expecting to get pulled out, but instead, I felt something getting pulled over me and was in silence for quite some time. While I was left alone, I tried everything in my power to get untied or make some sort of noise. It seemed like I was struggling for thirty minutes before I heard a bunch of screaming. I got anxious at that point. I tried making some commotion in case someone heard me, but this was not the case. I hit my head while trying to move and got knocked out cold again.

I was asleep when I heard the car door again. Before starting to move again, this person removed the blanket and bag from my face. I gave them the death stare. He removed a bottle of alcohol from a bag. I was too tired to try and figure out what kind it was. Before I knew it, though, I got forced to drink whatever it was. I tried to refuse, but this person was holding my mouth open. It was so unpleasant that once he got done making me drink that I got sick all over myself. When this person saw this, he covered me up and left me like that for the remainder of our trip. I felt disgusting, which led me to fall back asleep.

I slept peacefully until the person grabbed me and dragged me to a building. Once we got to what seemed like a door, I heard another person speak. It sounded like an older person because the voice was a lot deeper. I couldn't quite understand the whole conversation that was said, but the things I did hear I didn't like the sound of it.

"Take care of her, or the deal is off."

"Don't worry about it. This young lady will be in good hands. Did you do what you said you would?"

"Yes, but there is one problem."

"What would that be?"

"She got sick all over herself, so now she needs to be cleaned."

"I don't think clothes will be a huge problem with what we are going to be doing."

"Sounds great. I will see you in a week in half."

"Okay."

After the conversation, I was taken up a set of stairs and tied to a bedpost. The bag got taken off of my face. This new person was a tall male with brown eyes and dressed in all black clothing. He made sure I could see his eyes but nothing else.

"Now listen to me. I know you are Lily and you are supposed to be attending Juilliard for their dance program, I know you're a phenomenal dancer. I've been watching you for a while now. You don't know me, but you have heard of me. I am going to stop you from ruining my life. You will dance for me, and if you don't, then I will make your life a living nightmare. Do you understand?"

"Whoever you are, you will be caught. I can promise you won't get away with this. If I'm lucky, the police are already on the search."

"No one will ever find you. You are such a beautiful girl that you will be perfect for what I want. I hope you are ready for fun."

"What do you want from me? Who are you?"

"As I have mentioned before, I want you as my dancer. Do I make myself clear?"

"Yes, but you are going to have a difficult time making me do what you want. I don't do things on demand or forcefully."

"Then I see we are going to have a hard time keeping you alive."

"Whatever you say."

"We will give this a try. I am going to leave the room for exactly ten minutes, and when I get back, you are to be in the outfit that is on the bed, and already dancing. If you do not listen, there will be punishment. I dare you not to listen."

He then shut the door and left me all alone in a room with nothing but a bed with an outfit and a dresser. The outfit was a crop top with shorts that were booty shorts. There was no way on earth I was putting the costume on to expose my body to some stranger. I didn't realize how fast ten minutes went by because before I knew it, I heard the door opening. I quickly ran and hid under the bed, all curled up like a ball afraid of what was going to happen next.

When the guy opened the door, I knew he saw the clothes that weren't on my body because he said, "That little girl is going to have to learn her lesson." There wasn't any place for me to hide, so it was pretty easy to find me. When he saw me, he pulled me out and slapped me hard. He knocked me out, and when I woke up, I couldn't even remember my name.

Chapter 20

When I woke up, this person took his full advantage since he knew I couldn't remember anything. I got another bottle of alcohol forced down, but this time the person made sure that I didn't get sick by making me drink some water. Once the whole bottle was gone, I started to doze off again, but I didn't get the chance. I got forced to stand up. Once I was stable, there was music that started playing. Without thinking, I began to dance because the song sounded like Jingle Bell Rock, and whenever that played, I had to dance to it. I made a promise to myself after Mrs. Marine died that I would always dance to our song. I must have been doing something right because the slappings stopped for about ten minutes, but once I made a move he didn't like, I got slapped again. When twenty minutes were up, he let me stop.

"You have ten minutes to rest, and then it is right back at it. Do you understand?"

"Yes, sir. First, can I have something to eat? I'm starving."

"Sorry. We have nothing here. Better luck next time."

Right when he said that, my stomach growled loudly. I clenched my stomach tightly. He walked out of the room. I tried crawling around the room to see if I could find any crumbs or anything to eat. Unfortunately, this guy kept the place spotless. I guess that was one of his tactics for him not being found. I didn't even know what he looked like except that he has brown eyes. Other than that, I barely knew anything. As I was crawling around, he came back into the room. I didn't realize he came back up until he pulled me up and pushed me against the wall. I couldn't feel anything below my neck. So I, unfortunately, had to put up with everything the person was doing to me.

"I see you have been busy while I was away. Well, the fun is over now. You will dance again for me."

"What if I don't want to dance for you again? I already danced once for you."

"I don't care if you don't want to. You are my dancer and will dance for me whenever I want you to."

"No! I refuse to. My body is mine, and I already disrespected it once, and I will not do it again."

"Fine. You deserve what I'm about to do to you."

He slapped me again, but this time he knocked me out. I was out cold for a while. I didn't know the exact amount of time, but I know it was enough time for this guy to pick me up and take me to another location. When I woke up again, it looked like I was in a cellar of some sort. It was dark, cold, wet, and isolated. I tried yelling, but all I got in response was an echo of my voice.

I started crying. All I wanted was to get out of this situation and be with Amiah. I didn't even care about missing classes at Juilliard. I just wanted to be back at my comfy little apartment with my best friend. Right when I started crying, the guy came in.

"Are you willing to dance for me now?"

"In your dreams!"

"Okay then, you won't see the sun again."

"Whatever."

He left me again, all alone in the cellar. I didn't know what to think about this. I mean, it was better than being beaten up, but I was still scared. Right when I was about to give up hope of living, I heard something dripping. I got myself up and tried walking to see if I could find the source of the sound. I kept falling, though, since I was weak and couldn't even feel my legs. I hadn't eaten anything in the past two days. I also had very little water, which I assumed wasn't right for my health. It took me a good thirty minutes to get somewhat close to the noise. It sounded like it was right above me, but when I looked, I couldn't see anything but darkness. I then started to hear a very faint voice.

"Over here. Please help me." I could barely hear or distinguish if it were a guy or a girl. I walked for another five minutes until I finally found the voice.

"Oh my gosh, are you okay? Who are you? How long have you been here?"

"My name is Ann. I'm not okay. I'm not sure how long I have been here. I want to go home. I'm starving and thirsty. I don't know how much longer I can live. The person that captured me has kept some expired food back here, and the only water I receive is from over there." Ann pointed to a place on the ceiling. There was a leak in the roof as big as an over-ripened apple. It must have been raining outside because the rain kept coming down like there was no tomorrow. I decided to take my chance and find a bucket or something and fill it with water for both Ann and me. She was so dehydrated, and so was I. I needed to help keep her alive so she could help me figure out who this person was. I laid right there with Ann and tried to keep her company. She could barely talk anymore, so I just laid there, making sure she felt safe. It was going to be my mission to help her escape as well and keep her healthy. After about ten minutes, I heard the man yelling again.

"Lily. Where are you? You can run, but you can't hide."

I saw a light coming towards me, and I decided to run but carry Ann with me. She wasn't huge, and so I needed to hide her. I had no idea what this man did to her, but I was going to make sure he didn't get to her again. I knew I probably wouldn't get far, but I had to try at least. The running lasted for about two and a half minutes with Ann. I hid her behind a tall stack of boxes.

"Stay here and be quiet. I will come back to you. I promise."

"Okay," Ann said in a whimpering voice.

I kept running and hid behind another couple of boxes, about twenty feet away from Ann. I was surprisingly able to fit inside a box. I quickly got in and stayed still. I could hear the man, and he was getting frustrated because he couldn't find me.

"Where are you? I will find you, and you will regret it."

I could hear him kicking boxes and cursing under his breath. Saying things like "These damn girls will pay for my time." It was only a matter of time until he kicked my box. I was right about that. Once he kicked my box he tilted the box and pulled me out.

"You thought you could get away from me, didn't you? Well, you are wrong. I told you that you wouldn't be able to escape. Now you are going to pay for what you just pulled."

"Can't be any worse than what you have already done to me."

I knew right when I said that I was going to regret it. The man then pushed me against the wall and pulled my pants down. What he did next was unimaginable. I tried to squirm away, but he had a firm grip against me, making sure that I wasn't going anywhere. As he was forcing me to have sex with him, I kept crying out in pain. The torture went on for five minutes. I must have made a lot of noise that triggered something with Ann because she came out of her hiding spot and tried to stop him.

"Get off of her! She doesn't deserve this!"

"It's you. I thought you would have been dead by now. Well, if I can't do this to Lily, then it looks like I'm going to have to do this."

He pushed me to the ground, and went over to Ann. I couldn't believe that. I knew I tried to stop him by kicking him. I grabbed Ann and we ran. I picked her up because she couldn't run all that fast, and we got somewhat out of the cell, but he caught up to us when we were about to leave the front door.

"Where do you two think you are going? You two are mine!" He then grabbed us and took us back to the cell and then he put us in these cages. We were in two separate ones, and he locked them to make sure we weren't going to be able to escape. I didn't want to see what was going to happen next.

Chapter 21

Ann and I were in those cages for a long time. I lost track of time. It was easy, though, when there was no way to tell day from night in the cell. I occasionally knew I could hear church bells in the distance. They would ring once a day. I started to keep track, but I lost count after a hundred. Each day shortly after the bell, the guy would come in, force me to drink alcohol, rape me, and beat me until I was out cold. He did give me some water every couple of days to keep me barely alive. We would also get a piece of bread twice a day, but that's it. Each time the guy would leave I would find a way to pick the locks of the cages to escape, and then whenever I would hear the guy coming back, I would get back in the cage like nothing had happened. I couldn't ever escape the cellar due to the fact that the guy would lock the door of the cellar from the outside with padlocks.

One day after the bell rang, I was expecting the same thing as I have gotten in the past. Instead, though, the man didn't come in. It was a girl that looked just as bad as I did, but she was awake. I tried to talk to her, but I didn't have much luck.

"Hi. My name is Lily. What's yours?"

I got nothing but a stare and a couple of tears. I went over to the new girl to try and clean her face a little bit. After a few minutes of silence, she finally spoke out.

"Hi. My name is Angel. How long have you been down here?"

"I'm not sure how long I've been here. Let me tell you it's terrible here. I've been trying to find a way to escape since day one. He barely gives us any food or water. How many days have you been in his possession before he brought you down here?"

"I'm not exactly sure. I think like two days or something like that. It was hard to keep track of the days."

"I understand that."

"Yeah. You look horrible, Lily. What has he done to you?"

"He has raped me every single day. When I refuse to dance for him, he beats me until I'm out cold."

"That sounds horrible. Why would the strange man beat you when you don't dance for him?"

"He does it because he knows I'm a dancer, and I'm good at it as well."

"You are a dancer too?"

"Yes, I am a dancer. I'm supposed to be attending Juilliard for their dance program."

"No way! I'm a dancer as well, and I'm also supposed to be attending Juilliard."

"That is so awesome! If we ever get out of this place, maybe we can dance together."

"That would be awesome, Lily. I know we will be great friends once we get out of here."

"I know we will, Angel. Now we have to get out of here some way. We have to get help for this other girl, Ann, too. I honestly don't think she is still alive, but she is over there in the other cage."

Angel looked over to see Ann. She went over to the cage to check for a pulse.

"I'm afraid you are right, Lily. She didn't make it."

"I figured, but we need to find a way out for both Ann and us, so her family can get some justice."

"I know we do, but how?"

"I have no idea."

Right when I finished saying that, the door opened again. This time not one guy came in, but two guys came in. Each guy grabbed one of us girls. They not only forced us to have sex with them, but they also beat us again. The rape went on for a good hour and a half. After they got done, they switched girls. The guy that hit me first went to Angel, and the guy that had Angel came to me. Again another hour and a half went by. When they got done, we both got pushed to the ground while crying. The guys left the room, and we were left alone with our thoughts. Bruises were left all over our bodies. We both crawled into each other's arms and tried to comfort each other. It only took five minutes for us to fall asleep, but the last thing Angel said to me was, "I'll always be your friend, Lily." That was what made me fall asleep with a smile on my face. If I had known that was the last time I was going to see her for a while, I would have made it last.

Chapter 22

When I woke up again, I was in another different place. This place was different by actually having light. I turned on the light and tried to walk around, but by this time, I was so weak I could barely walk, speak, or move any part of my body. I tried to yell my loudest for Angel, but the only response I got was a rat family scurrying across the floor looking for food, I assume. I was usually terrified of rats, but because of my weakness, I didn't have the motivation to move or yell. I was exhausted and started to accept the fact that I was going to die, so I better die in my sleep. I made an effort to open the door that was five feet away from me to see where it led me. To my surprise, it led me to a church auditorium.

I couldn't believe it. I finally figured out who had Angel and me in their possession. It was the guy that Maddy had told me about that takes young girls and keeps them for a year. I didn't want to believe her, but I should have. I couldn't think he was going after dancers now, or at least I thought that was his pattern. I went and crawled to the very first pew. I laid down, and right before I fell asleep, I heard the bells ring. It was a soothing noise now that I knew what they were. Shortly after that, I fell asleep and slept the most peaceful sleep that I have slept in the past two weeks. I had to have slept at least nine hours because when I woke up, I couldn't believe who was with me. A bunch of strangers surrounded me and I shouted at the top of my lungs. I thought this was a nightmare that would never end.

A lot of them looked curious, but there was one individual that saw me and had this face of relief.

"Is your name Lily? Have you been missing for a while?"

"Yes, I'm Lily, and I have been missing for months. Who are you?"

"My name is Pastor Greene. I am a friend of your parents. Your mom called me about seven months ago to tell me how you have been missing and wanted prayers. I told her that I wouldn't only pray, but I would also help look for you. After I was done in the church office each day, I spent at least three hours looking for you, and asking people if they have seen you. Nobody within fifty miles has seen you. I was about to give up hope, but then I came into the church today and found you sleeping. How did you end up here?"

"Honestly, it's a little blurry because I have so much alcohol in my system that I can't remember everything. The only thing I can think of happening is a man in all black kidnapping me from my apartment and driving me to a mysterious place. He then gave me to another man all dressed in black, who forced me to dance, raped me, and then I was beaten. I haven't eaten or drank anything in a couple of days. I did meet another girl, Angel. She was another girl who got kidnapped. Is she here as well? Did you save her? You guys have too! She is going to be attending Juilliard as well. I want her here with me."

"I'm sorry, Lily, we haven't found anyone else here. I will have someone call the police to let them know that you are alive and okay. They are still looking for Angel. Do you have any details of where you were? Anything will help."

"All I can recall is being in a bedroom with only a bed and a dresser. The room was spotless as well. After the bedroom, I got taken to some sort of cellar. It was huge but isolated. In that cellar I was raped and beaten with barely any food or water. I was there for over one hundred days with the same

166

things happening. Yesterday I was brought here, though. That is why you found me sleeping on a pew."

"I'm so sorry to hear all of this, Lily. We need to get you to the hospital right away. I will call your mom on the way. When she heard that you were missing, both her, your father and your sister caught the next flight here. They have been staying in a hotel near your apartment. They have been worried sick."

"I can imagine. I can't wait to see everyone again. I thought it would never happen. I can't wait to see Amiah as well! I know she isn't doing well without me."

"I know they can't wait to see you. Now let's go."

"Okay."

The drive to the hospital was about fifteen minutes. When we pulled into the parking lot, I saw my parents and sister! I staggered up to them to give them a huge hug.

"Lily, you are alive," both my parents said at the same time.

"Yes, I am alive and lucky to be. I went through so much that I thought the next time you guys saw me would be in a wooden box."

"Oh, Lily. I warned you to be careful. I'm glad you are safe, though."

"I know, Maddy. I'm sorry. I should've listened to you better. Now I know I should always listen."

"It's okay, Lily. The only thing that matters is you are safe. Now let's go get you checked out."

"Okay."

As we were walking in, I got nervous in my stomach because I wasn't sure what to expect.

When we were in the back room waiting, my parents were telling me stories. Once the doctor came in and I told them what happened, they made me take a pregnancy test. I was so worried about what the results were going to come back as. The whole time taking the test, my heart was beating as fast as a rocket. When done with the test, I went back into the room with my parents. We were all laughing when the doctors came back in.

"Lily, can you remember if the person that raped you used protection or not?"

"There were two different people that raped me. I think one of them used protection, but the other one did not."

"Okay, because I'm afraid to tell you that you are pregnant. You are three weeks along."

Right when I received the news, there were tears in my eyes.

Chapter 23

"There is no way I am pregnant! I am not ready to be a mom. I have my whole future ahead of me."

Amiah came rushing in and comforted me. "Lily, I am so sorry that this happened to you. I will be here with you through everything."

"It doesn't matter, Amiah. My whole future got thrown out the window. I already missed my first year at Juilliard. I truly doubt that Mrs. Bean will still let me come back to classes. I can bet you that she already thinks I am just like Maddy now."

"I truly don't think Mrs. Bean thinks that of you."

When Amiah said that Mrs. Bean came walking into the hospital room. I couldn't do anything but cry when I saw her.

"Are you okay, Lily? I was worried sick about you."

"I'm fine, but I have some news for you."

"What is it, Lily?" Mrs. Bean asked.

"I got raped, and so the person who raped me didn't use protection, and now I'm pregnant."

"Oh, Lily. You will be okay. We are all here for you."

"Thank you for that."

Mrs. Bean started crying. "We missed you this year, but clearly, it isn't your fault. I still want to offer my scholarship to you, but I was thinking you could take a year off and go home with your parents. This way, you can take care of yourself and the baby. When next fall comes around, you can come back. I want you to take care of yourself and stay safe. How does that sound?"

"The deal sounds great. Thank you, Mrs. Bean."

A couple of days after that, I got released from the hospital. The next nine months were going to be a challenge for everyone, including me.

ABOUT THE AUTHOR

Skylar L. Hill is an ordinary young lady who has gone through similar struggles that most might not see that she has gone through. She writes in her free time has a way to express her feelings. Skylar will always continue to write whether that be short stories, novellas, children's stories, or novels. She loves traveling and helping those around her. When an opportunity comes up to travel and explore she takes the chance no matter if there is a risk involved. She considers everyone's feelings but in the end she does what she wants because she only has to please God and herself. She is a Christian and tries her best to incorporate Christianity into her writing whenever possible.

Also available by Skylar L. Hill

Everywhere I Go

Julie Scranton's life was happy and ordinary until her parents split up when she was 14. After suffering under her abusive mother for several years, she finally decides to run away and locate the father she has not seen since he left. Follow her on this physical, emotional and spiritual journey, where she finds much that she never expected to.

Also available from Bob Scott Publishing

The Redemption of Soul Dallas
Cara Jordan White

Eighteen and homeless, Soul Dallas has more to worry about than what he'll be doing this New Year's. In a town where compassion is rare and malice plenty, he's left for dead by a gang seeking revenge for his father's debts.

When anxiety-burdened Lana provides him with shelter, she's swept into his world of pandemonium where fear means fight not flight. Leaving behind her imprisoned life with an over-bearing mother, she learns of Soul's shocking past and what it truly means to be alive. But when the gang closes ranks and Soul falls ill, finding a bright future seems futile.

Together Soul and Lana must seek reason behind an ally's betrayal, a dead woman's return, and the ruthlessness behind some people's need for vengeance.

But the pair don't always see eye to eye, and each have plans that could jeopardize everything.

www.facebook.com/TheRedemptionOfSoulDallas